Congregation of the Holy Rosary

The rule of Saint Augustine

The constitutions of the Sisters of Penance

Congregation of the Holy Rosary

The rule of Saint Augustine
The constitutions of the Sisters of Penance

ISBN/EAN: 9783741183287

Manufactured in Europe, USA, Canada, Australia, Japa

Cover: Foto ©Andreas Hilbeck / pixelio.de

Manufactured and distributed by brebook publishing software
(www.brebook.com)

Congregation of the Holy Rosary

The rule of Saint Augustine

THE

RULE OF SAINT AUGUSTINE

AND THE

Constitutions of the Sisters of Penance

OF THE

THIRD ORDER OF SAINT DOMINIC.

FORMING THE

Congregation of the Most Holy Rosary

OF THE UNITED STATES OF AMERICA.

MOTHER-HOUSE AND NOVITIATE,
At Sinsinawa Mound, Grant County, Wisconsin.
1889.

PREFACE.

THE Rule of St. Augustine is taken from a letter written by the Saint to a Convent of Nuns under his jurisdiction. The Epistle bears the number 211, and also 109, in the Edition of the Benedictines, Paris, 1688.

The Community of Sisters of the Third Order of St. Dominic, bearing the name of Congregation of the Most Holy Rosary of the United States of America, from its foundation. in 1846, by Very Rev. F. B. Samuel Charles Mazzuchelli, at that time Commissary Provincial of the Order of Preachers in these United States, has followed the Constitutions of the Third Order, compiled by him, with the approval of Most Rev. F. B. Thomas Ancarani, Master-General of the Order, and, in 1859, of Most Rev. F. B. Alexander Vincent Jandel, Master-General of the Order. This compendium of the Constitutions, the text of which was supplemented and explained by full and most lucid commentaries of the venerable compiler, under his wise, holy, and paternal guidance, sufficed for the needs of the Community, and for many years after his death. Subsequently, the rapid growth of the Community, the establishment of many and distant Branch Houses, yearly increasing in number, and in various Dioceses, rendered necessary this more complete work. It has been drawn chiefly from the edition approved in

1877, for the use of the Congregation of the Third Order, at Stone, England.

In 1877, Sisters duly authorized by the Chapter of our Congregation, visited Rome, and after an audience with the Holy Father, Pius Ninth of blessed memory, assisted by the counsel and direction of Most Rev. F. B. Joseph Maria San Vito, Vicar-General of the Order, proceeded to complete the design of compiling this work. The Master-General of the Order, Most Rev. F. B. Joseph Maria Larroca, visiting our Mother-House in 1881, was pleased to give it his paternal blessing and approval, urging the utmost rapidity, consistent with care and prudence.

In 1887 this body of Constitutions was submitted to His Paternity, who placed it in the hands of Most Rev. F. B. Marcolino Cicognani, Procurator-General of the Order, who, throughout the whole compilation, has assisted and encouraged it with counsels, direction and most paternal and affectionate solicitude, and to whom this entire Congregation owes a debt of gratitude which may never be forgotten.

The Most Rev. Procurator-General laid the work before the Sacred Congregation of the Propagation of the Faith early in the year 1888, and on the 29th day of July of that same year, this Congregation of the M. H. Rosary, and these Constitutions with emendations and additions from the hand of the Most Rev. Proc.-General, received the approbation of the Holy See, in the following Decree, dated the 17th day of August.

The letter of the Most Rev. Proc.-General conveying this Decree, contains these words of explanation :

" Questa approvazine *ad triennium* è una ceremonia, perchè mai suole la S. Cgne. dare delle Costituzioni la prima volta definitiva approvazione." " This approbation for three years is a formality, because the Sacred Congregation is never accustomed to give definite approbation to Constitutions the first time." Therefore, in obedience to the Most Rev. Procurator-General of the Order, these Constitutions were ordered to be printed with the Decree *ad triennium*, with space provided for insertion at the end of that period, of the Final Decree.

DECRETUM.

Superiorissa Generalis Sororum Dominicanarum Tertii Ordinis Pœnitentiæ ex Congregatione S S'mi Rosarii in Statibus Fœderatis Americæ Septentrionalis a S* Congregatione de Propaganda Fide iam ante approbationem sive Instituti sive Constitutionum enixis precibus expóstulavit. Porro cum prædicta Congregatio late diffusa, et Constitutionum observantia ac religioso spiritu floreat, uberesque fructus divinâ afflante gratiâ retulerit, commissio consultorum, cui munus novas Congregationes ac Constitutiones examinandi demandatum est diё 12 Julii 1888, praeside Eminentissimo Cardinali Camillo Mazzella, re mature perpensa, attentisque literis testimonialibus plurium Episcoporum, qui has Sorores Sacræ Congregationi de Propaganda Fide commendarunt, præfatum Institutum definitive, Constitutiones vero ad triennium per modum experimenti approbandas censuit introductis nonnullis correctionibus et modificationibus, uæ in adnexo exemplari adnotantur.

Hanc vero resolutionem Commissionis in audientia diei 29 Julii, 1888, Ssmo D. N., Leoni XIII. a Ro. P*. Do. Dominico Jacobini Archiepiscopo Tyrensi et S. Congregationis de Propaganda Fide a Secretis relatam, Sanctitas Sua approbare ac super his præsens Decretum expediri mandavit.

Datum Romæ ex Ædibus S. C. de Prop'da Fide die 17 Augusti, An. MDCCCLXXXVIII.

[Loc. Sig]   Joannes Card. Simeoni Præfectus.

Pro. Secretario, Zephyrinus Zitelli, S. Off.

DECREE.

The Superioress General of the Dominican Sisters of the Third Order of Penance, of the Congregation of the Most Holy Rosary in the United States of North America, has before, with earnest prayers, petitioned the Sacred Congregation of the Propagation of the Faith for the approbation whether of the Institute or the Constitutions. Moreover, since the aforesaid Congregation being widely diffused, flourishes under the observance of the Constitutions and its religious spirit and hath produced abundant fruits through the inspiration of Divine grace, the Committee of Consultors, to whom is entrusted the office of examining new Congregations and Constitutions, on the 12th day of July, 1888, His Eminence Cardinal Camillo Mazzella, presiding, the affair having been maturely considered, and regard being had to the testimonial letters of many Bishops who have commended these Sisters to the Sacred Congregation of the Propagation of the

Faith, resolved that the aforesaid Institute should receive Final Approval, but the Constitutions should be approved for three years, by way of trial, certain corrections and modifications being inserted which are noted in the adjoined copy. Moreover, in an audience of the 29th day of July, 1888, this decision of the Committee, having been laid before our Most Holy Lord, Leo XIII., by Most Rev. Dominico Jacobini, Archbishop of Tyre, and Secretary of the Sacred Congregation of the Propagation of the Faith, His Holiness approved it and commanded the present Decree to be expedited to that effect.

Given at Rome, from the Sacred Congregation of Propaganda, on the 17th day of August, 1888.

Joannes Card. Simeoni, Praefectus.

[Seal.]

Pro Secretary,
Zephyrinus Zitelli,
S. Off.

FINAL DECREE.

TABLE OF CONTENTS.

PAGE.

RULE OF ST. AUGUSTINE - - - - - - 17
CONSTITUTIONS OF THE SISTERS OF PENANCE OF THE
 THIRD ORDER OF ST. DOMINIC - - - - 33

PROLOGUE.

Section 1. Of the Constitutions - - - - 33
Section 2. Of the Institution and Character of the
    Order and of this Congregation - - 34
Section 3. Of the Obligation of these Constitu-
    tions and of Dispensations - - 36
Section 4. Of Customs - - - - - 41

PART FIRST.

OF THE FORM OF OUR COMMUNITY LIFE, AND THE MAN-
 NER OF RECEPTION INTO THE CONGREGATION - - 43

CHAPTER I.

OF THE OFFICE AND OTHER SPIRITUAL EXERCISES - - 43
Section 1. Of Promptitude in going to Office - 43

Section 2. In what the Daily Office consists - - 44
Section 3. Of the Obligation of the Daily Office - 46
Section 4. Of the Manner of Reciting the Office
and of the Attention Required - - 47
Section 5. Of Mental Prayer - - - - 48
Section 6. Of Spiritual Reading - - - - 51
Section 7. Of the Annual Spiritual Retreat - - 51
Section 8. Of the Confraternities of the Holy
Rosary, of the Most Holy Name,
and of the Angelic Warfare - - 52
Section 9. Of various Ordinances relating to this
Chapter - - - - - 55

CHAPTER II.

Of the Inclinations - - - - - - 58
Section 1. Of the Inclinations in general - - 58
Section 2. How the Most Holy Sacrament is to
be adored on entering the Choir,
and of the Ceremonies of the
Office - - - - - - 59
Section 3. Of the three kinds of Inclinations - 61
Section 4. Of the two kinds of Genuflections - - 63
Section 5. Of the two kinds of Prostrations - - 65
Section 6. Of the times when the Sisters stand
facing the Altar; when they stand
facing Choir to Choir; and when
they sit down - - - - - 67

CHAPTER III.

Of the Suffrages for the Dead - - - - 69

CHAPTER IV.

Of Confession, of Mass and Holy Communion - - 73
  Section 1. Of Confession - - - - - 73
  Section 2. Of Mass and Holy Communion - - 74

CHAPTER V.

Of Fasting and Abstinence - - - - - 76

CHAPTER VI.

Of the Refectory - - - - - - - 78
  Section 1. Of the Meals and Manner of Serving
          at Table - - - - - 78
  ection 2. Of Reading at Table - - - - 82

CHAPTER VII.

Of the Work - - - - - - - - 84

CHAPTER VIII.

Of the Sick - - - - - - - - 86

CHAPTER IX.

Of the Beds, the Dormitories and the Cells - - 88

CHAPTER X.

OF THE HABIT - - - - - - - - 90

  Section 1. Of the Habit of the Order - - - 90

  Section 2. Of the Obligation of Superiors to supply their subjects with clothing, and of the Habit Room - - - 91

  Section 3. Of the Dress of the Children educated in our Convents - - - - 93

CHAPTER XI.

OF THE SCHOOLS AND THE OBLIGATIONS OF THE TEACHERS - - - - - - - - 94

  Section 1. Of the Obligations of the Teachers in General - - - - - 94

  Section 2. Of the Boarding School - - - 99

CHAPTER XII.

OF LETTERS - - - - - - - - - 101

CHAPTER XIII.

OF SILENCE AND THE PARLOR - - - - 104

  Section 1. Of Silence - - - - - 104

  Section 2. Of the Parlor and of Relations with Externs - - - - - - 108

CHAPTER XIV.

OF THOSE WHO SHALL BE RECEIVED - - - - 112

  Section 1. Of Postulants - - - - - 112

Section 2. Of the property of Postulants and
         Novices - - - - - - 115
Section 3. Of the lawful manner of receiving to
         the Habit - - - - - 119

CHAPTER XV.

Of the Novices and of their Instruction - - 123
Section 1. Of the Novitiate - - - - - 123
Section 2. Of the Mistress of Novices - - 126
Section 3. Of the Instruction of the Novices - - 128
Section 4. Of the Term of Probation - - - 134

CHAPTER XVI.

Of Profession - - - - - - - 139
Section 1. Of the Form of Profession and of the
         Nature of the Vows - - - 139
Section 2. Of Poverty and Community of Goods 141
Section 3. Of Chastity and Enclosure - - - 148
Section 4. Of Obedience - - - - - 151

CHAPTER XVII.

Of Faults - - - - - - - - 156
Section 1. Of light Faults - - - - 156
Section 2. Of middle Faults - - - - 158
Section 3. Of grievous Faults - - - - 160
Section 4. Of more grievous Faults - - - 163
Section 5. Of the manner of proceeding against
         those guilty of more grievous Faults 167
Section 6. Of the most grievous Fault - - 169
Section 7. Of Apostates - - - - - 170

CHAPTER XVIII.

OF THE CHAPTER OF FAULTS - - - - - 172
  Section 1. Of the Obligation of holding Chapter, and its importance for regular discipline - - - - - - 172
  Section 2. Of the manner of holding the Chapter of Faults - - - - - 177

PART SECOND.

OF THE GOVERNMENT OF THE CONGREGATION - - 180

CHAPTER I.

OF THE AMERICAN CONGREGATION OF THE MOST HOLY ROSARY - - - - - - - - 180

CHAPTER II.

OF THE MOTHER GENERAL - - - - - 182
  Section 1. Of the Office and Authority of the Mother General - - - - 182
  Section 2. Of the Election of the Mother General 184
  Section 3. Of those who are eligible to the Office of Mother General - - - - 193
  Section 4. Of the duration and cessation of the Office of Mother General - - 194
  Section 5. Of the duties of the Mother General - 197

Section 6. Of the Vicaress of the Mother
General - - - - - 202
Section 7. Of the Appointment of the Sisters - 203
Section 8. Of Visitation - - - - - 206

CHAPTER III.

Of the Council of the Congregation - - - 209

CHAPTER IV.

Of the General Chapter - - - - - 216

Section 1. Of those who have a voice in the
General Chapter and of the time of
its celebration - - - - 216
Section 2. Of the Associate of the Conventual
Prioress - - - - - 217
Section 3. Of what is to be done throughout the
Congregation at the approach of the
General Chapter - - - - 223
Section 4. Of what is to be done in the Convent
where the Chapter is held, immedi-
ately before its celebration - - 225
Section 5. Of the Election of the Diffinitresses - 226
Section 6. Of the manner of celebrating the
General Chapter - - - - 230
Section 7. Of the acts of the General Chapter - 234
Section 8. Of the Intermediate Assembly - - 236
Section 9. Of Precedence - - - - 237

CHAPTER V.

Of the Bursar General - - - - - 240

CHAPTER VI.

Of the Archives of the Congregation   -   -   - 244

CHAPTER VII.

Of Foundations -   -   -   -   -   -   - 246
Of the necessary conditions for the erection of a
        Convent   -   -   -   -   - 246

CHAPTER VIII.

Of the Conventual Prioress   -   -   -   - 250
Section 1. Of the Institution ot the Conventual
        Prioress -   -   -   -   -   - 250
Section 2. Of the authority and duties of the
        Conventual Prioress   -   -   - 250
Section 3. Of the Vicaress of a House not yet
        erected into a Priory   -   -   - 260
Section 4. Of the Conventual Council   -   - 261
Section 5. Of the Conventual Chapter   -   - 265
Section 6. Of the Sub-Prioress   -   -   - 266
Section 7. Of the Syndica -   -   -   -   - 270
Section 8. Of the Deposit, the Depositaries, and
        other Officials of the Convent   - 273.
Section 9. Of the Archives and Inventories of the
        Convents   -   -   -   -   - 277
Section 10. Of Traveling   -   -   -   - 279
Section 11. Of Sisters who are visiting Convents
        where they are not assigned, and of
        Guests -   -   -   -   -   - 280
Section 12. Of the Annals   -   -   -   - 282

THE RULE OF ST. AUGUSTINE.

THE following are the things, dearest Sisters, which we command you who are assembled in the Monastery to observe.

The first purpose for which you have been brought together is, that you dwell in unity in the house, and that you have but one soul and one heart in God; and call not anything your own, but let all things be common. Let food and clothing be distributed to each one of you by your Superioress, not in equal measure to all, because you are not all of equal strength, but so as to provide for each one according to her need. For thus you read in the Acts of the Apostles, that they had all things common, and that distribution was made to every man according as he had need. Let those who had possessions in the world freely consent, when they enter the Monastery, that they should be for the common use. And as for those who possessed nothing, let them not expect to have in the Monastery those things which they were not able to procure in the world. Nevertheless, in case of infirmity, let them also be supplied with all that they require, even though their poverty was such in the world that they were unable to obtain even necessaries. But let not these consider themselves happy because they have found such food and raiment as they could not have obtained in the world; neither let them lift up their heads because they are become the companions of those whom they would not have presumed to approach when in the world; but let them rather lift up their hearts to Heaven, and not seek after the goods of this world; lest Monasteries become useful to the rich, but not to the poor, the rich being there humbled, whilst the poor are puffed up. On the other hand, let not those who seemed to be somewhat in the world, despise their Sisters who came from poverty into this holy society; but let them endeavor to glory, not in the dignity of their rich parents, but in the society of their poorer Sisters. Neither let them be lifted up if they have bestowed any of their possessions on the Community, nor glory more in their riches because they are sharing them in the Monastery, than if they were enjoying them in the world. For every other kind of iniquity brings forth evil works; but pride lies lurking even in good works, that it may destroy them. For of what profit is it to have distributed her goods to the poor, and to have become poor herself, if the wretched soul be made more proud in her contempt of riches than she was in their possession? Be, therefore, all of one mind, and live in concord, and honor God in one another, whose temples you have been made.

Be instant in prayer at the hours and times appointed. In the Oratory, let no one do anything excepting that for which it was made, and from which it derives its name; so that if, by chance, any should wish to pray out of the appointed hours (if they have leisure), there may be none to disturb them by being employed there in any other occupation. When you pray to God in psalms and hymns, meditate in your heart on that which you utter with your voice. And do not sing except what you find appointed to be sung; but what is not appointed must not be sung.

Subdue your flesh by fasting, and abstinence from meat and drink, as far as your health permits. But when any one is not able to fast, let her, however, take no food out of meals, unless she be sick. When you go to table, listen without noise and contention to that which is read to you according to custom, until you rise from your meal; nor let your mouth only receive food, but let your ears also be fed with the Word of God. If any are treated differently from the rest, as to food, because they are weak from a former habit of living, it must not disquiet nor seem unjust to those whom different habits have rendered stronger. Neither let them think their companions more fortunate, because they are allowed more; but rather let them congratulate themselves, because their strength is greater. And if to those who came to the Monastery after a more delicate nurture, any food, raiment or covering be given which is not allowed to those who are stronger and therefore happier, these last must consider how much the others have already come down from their secular way of living, although they have not attained to the same austerity of life as those who are of a more robust constitution. Neither must the rest be disquieted, because they see a few indulged (not to pay them any honor, but to support their weakness), lest that odious abuse arise in the Monastery, of making the rich endure hardships, whilst the poor are allowed to become delicate. As it is better for those who are actually sick to take less food, that they be not overloaded by it; so after their sickness, they must be treated in such a manner that they may recover their strength as soon as possible; even though they have come from the humblest state of poverty in the world; because their recent sickness has produced in them the same weakness which former habits of life have produced in the rich. But when they have recovered their former strength, let them return to their more austere but happier way of living (for the less the servants of God require, the better it becomes them), lest their will should attach itself to those indulgences when recovered, which were really necessary for them in sickness. Let those consider themselves the richest, who are the best able to bear abstinence; for it is better to need less than to have more.

Let not your habit be singular, neither let it

be your aim to please by your dress, but by
your behavior. When you go out, walk together; when you have arrived at the place
where you are going, remain together. Let
there be nothing in your gait, in your manner,
in your dress or in any of your movements,
which can tempt any. one to evil; but let your
whole demeanor be such as becomes the sanctity of your state. If your eyes light upon any
man, let them never be fixed upon him. When
you go out, you are not forbidden to see men;
but to try to attract them, or to wish to
be admired by them, is criminal. For not
only by touch, but by affection, and by looks
also, mutual concupiscence arises. Say not
that your minds are pure, if your eyes be impure, because an impure eye is the messenger
of an impure heart. And when, though the
tongue be silent, the mutual looks of both par-
ties proclaim the impurity of their hearts, and
concupiscence moves them to take pleasure in
sinful desires, though their bodies remain invio-
late, yet is the virtue of chastity destroyed in
their souls. Neither must she who fixes her
eyes upon a man, and is pleased that his eyes
are fixed upon her, imagine that she is not per-

ceived by others when she does this. She is
perfectly seen, and by those by whom she
thinks she is not seen. But supposing that
her fault remained concealed and were per-
ceived by no one, how will she avoid Him who
looks down from above, whose eye nothing can
escape? Or is He to be supposed not to observe, because His patience is proportioned to
the greatness of His wisdom? Let, therefore,
the religious woman fear to displease Him,
lest she should desire unlawfully to please men.
Let her remember that He beholds all things,
that she may not, with evil intention, behold
men. For the fear of God in this matter is ·
commended, where it is written : " he who fixes
his eye is an abomination to the Lord." When,
therefore, you are together in a church or anywhere else where there are men, keep watch
mutually over each other's modesty ; for God,
who dwells in you, will, by this means, preserve
you from yourselves.

And if you perceive this liberty of the eye
in any one amongst you, admonish her of it
immediately, that the fault may not increase,
but may be corrected by her Sister's reproof.
But if immediately after the admonition, or at

any other time, you see her again do the same
thing, it is then necessary that whoever is
aware of it, should declare her wounded state,
that she may be healed.   Nevertheless point it
out first to one or two more, that by the mouth
of two or three she may be convicted and
punished with due severity.   And do not consider yourselves as guilty of ill-will when you
make this known.   On the contrary, you would
be really guilty if you were to permit your
Sisters to perish by keeping silence, when, by
exposing their fault, you might have corrected
them.   For if your Sister had a wound in her
body, which she would fain keep secret through
fear of an operation, would it not be cruelty in
you to conceal it, and true mercy to make it
known ?   How much more, then, ought you to
make this spiritual wound manifest, that its
corruption may not increase in the heart.   But
before the fault is pointed out to the others, by
whom she is to be convicted, in case she deny
it, it should be first told to the Superioress (if
being admonished, she neglect to amend) ; that,
if possible, being corrected by a private reproof,
her fault may be kept from the knowledge of
others.   But if she deny it, then the others are

to be brought forward, that, before the whole Community, she may not only be accused by one, but convicted by two or three witnesses. Being thus convicted, she must undergo an expiatory penance, according to the judgment of the Superioress, or of the Ecclesiastical Superior. If she refuse to bear this (even though she will not depart of her own accord), she must be expelled from your Community; not in cruelty, but in mercy, that she may not ruin others by the pestilential contagion of her example. And let all that I have said with respect to the fault of fixing the eyes, be diligently observed in discovering, forbidding, manifesting, proving and punishing other offenses, with charity towards the offender, and hatred against the sin. If any one shall have committed so great a fault as secretly to receive letters or presents from any one, if she confess it of her own accord, let her be forgiven, and let prayer be made for her. But if she be taken in the fault, and convicted, let her be severely corrected according to the judgment of the Superioress, or of your Ecclesiastical Superior

Your clothes shall be kept in one place, under the charge of one or two Sisters, or as

many as may be required to shake them out
often, to preserve them from the moth. And,
as you are fed from a common kitchen, so shall
you be clothed out of a common habit-room.
When clothes are given out to you according
to the season, concern yourselves as little as
possible whether you receive the same habit
which you took off, or one which another had
worn; provided only that no one be denied
what is necessary for her. But if contentions
and murmurs arise, and any one complain that
she has received a worse habit than she had
before, and that she is not considered worthy
to be clothed like the other Sisters, you prove
how wanting you are in that interior holy
raiment of the heart, when you thus contend
about the clothing of the body. However,
though in consideration of your weakness you
be allowed to receive the same habit as before,
yet, whatever you leave off, shall be kept in
one place, under the care of those who have
that charge; so that no one shall work anything for herself alone, whether it be for clothing, bedding, bed-clothes, girdles, kerchiefs and
the like, but all your work shall be done for
the common use, and that with greater zeal

and more cheerful diligence, than if you were each employed for yourselves only. For it is written of charity, that "it seeketh not its own," which means that charity prefers the general good to its own, not its own to the general good. And thus, the more you study the advantage of the Community in preference to your own, the more you may know that you advance in perfection: since charity, which abideth forever, has thus the pre-eminence over those things which only supply the transitory necessities of this life. Hence it follows, that when anyone shall bring to his daughters, or those in any way depending on him in the Monastery, clothing, or any other things that may be reckoned as necessaries, they must not be received secretly, but must be placed in the hands of the Superioress, that, being kept in the common stock, they may be given out to any one who may stand in need of them. And if any Sister shall conceal what is brought to her, let her be punished as guilty of theft.

Let your clothes be washed, according to the judgment of your Superioress, either by yourselves or others, but let not an excessive desire of clean clothing bring inward defilement on the soul. Let not the use of the bath be frequent among you, but if through infirmity any Sister shall require it oftener than usual, let it not be refused her. Let her have it without murmuring, according to the advice of the physician, so that (even if the patient be unwilling) by order of the Superioress, whatever is necessary for her health may be done. If, however, the Sister desire the bath and it be not good for her, let not her inclina tion be indulged. For sometimes that which is pleasant is believed to be of service though it be really injurious. Lastly, if any Sister have a secret pain in the body, let her, being the servant of God, be believed without mistrust when she declares what she suffers. But, nevertheless, if it be not certain that what she fancies is really the best means of removing the pain, let the physician be consulted. The Sisters must not go to the baths or anywhere else, when they are obliged to go, fewer than two or three together. And she who is obliged to go anywhere shall not choose her own companions, but must go with those whom the Superioress shall appoint. The care of the sick, either when recovering or when laboring under any infirmity (though without fever), must be committed to one Sister, who must ask from the kitchen whatever she shall find necessary for each. Those who have charge of the stores, or the habits, or the library, must serve their Sisters without murmuring. The books may be asked for at a certain hour every day. Whoever asks for them out of that hour must not have them. But clothing and shoes when required, must be given without delay, by those under whose charge they have been placed.

As for disputes, either avoid them altogether or bring them to an end as soon as possible, lest anger grow into hatred and make of a mote a beam, and cause the soul to be guilty of murder. For it was not written for mán only, " He that hateth his brother is a murderer," but the female sex also is included in the precept under the name of man, who was first created. Whosoever shall offend another by injurious words, or by upbraiding her with a fault, shall be careful as soon as possible to make amends for the offense, and the Sister who has been offended must forgive at once without dispute. But if they have mutually

offended each other. both must mutually forgive each other, on account of your prayers,
which the oftener you make the more holy
they should be. A Sister who, though often
tempted to anger, yet hastens to ask pardon of
the person whom she knows she has offended,
is better than one who is slower to be angry,
but is also slower to ask pardon. And a Sister
who never will ask pardon, or who does not ask
it from her heart, is unworthy of remaining in
the Monastery, even if she be not actually expelled from thence. Refrain, therefore, from
harsh words, but if such should escape your
lips, be not slow to let the remedy proceed
from the same tongue which inflicted the
wound. But when the necessity of discipline
compels such of you as are superiors to use
harsh words in reproving your inferiors, though
you should feel that you have gone too far in
so doing, it is nevertheless not required of you
to ask pardon of your subjects lest the authority
of your government be weakened through too
great regard to humility. But you must ask
pardon from the Lord of all, who knows how
much you love those very persons whom you
corrected more severely, perhaps, than was rea-

sonable. Yet the love that is between you
must not be sensual but spiritual.

Obey your Superioress as a mother, and yet
more your Ecclesiastical Superior, who has
charge of you all. It is more particularly the
office of the Superioress to see that all these
things are well observed; and if anything
should chance to be less well observed, she
must not allow it to be negligently passed over,
but must take care that it be amended and
corrected; and if any matter shall exceed her
capability, or the limits of her authority, she
must refer the case to the Ecclesiastical Superior. Let not your Superioress account herself happy, because she rules over you with
authority, but because she has the opportunity
of serving you with charity. As your Superioress, let her be in honor before men; but in
fear before God, let her lie prostrate at your
feet. Let her show herself an example of good
works to you all. Let her correct the dis-
orderly, comfort the dejected, support the weak,
and be patient with all. Let her be strict with
herself in the observance of religious discipline,
and cautious in exacting it of others. And although both love and fear be necessary, yet

must she rather desire to be loved than feared by you, ever remembering that she must give an account to God for you all. Be, therefore, the more obedient, out of compassion, not for yourselves only, but also for her, who is in so much more danger, in proportion as she is higher in authority over you.

The Lord grant that you observe all these things as becomes lovers of spiritual beauty, and those who are fragrant with the sweet odor of Christ through a good conversation ; not as slaves under the law, but as those who have been set free by grace. Now that you may see yourselves in this little book as in a mirror, and may neglect nothing through forgetfulness, let it be read to you once a week, and whenever you shall find yourselves to be in the practice of what it enjoins, give thanks to God the giver of all good. But whenever any one amongst you shall perceive that she has failed in any point, let her repent for the past and be on her guard for the future ; praying that her offenses may be forgiven, and that she be not led into temptation.

HERE ENDS THE RULE OF ST. AUGUSTINE

CONSTITUTIONS

OF THE

SISTERS OF PENANCE

OF THE

THIRD ORDER OF ST. DOMINIC,

FORMING THE CONGREGATION OF THE MOST HOLY ROSARY OF THE UNITED STATES OF AMERICA.

———

PROLOGUE.

———

SECTION I.

2. OF THE CONSTITUTIONS.

3. Forasmuch as we are commanded by our Rule to have one heart and one soul in the Lord, it is just that we, who live under one Rule, and are bound by vow to one profession, should be found uniform also in all observance

of Religion in order that the outward uniformity of our practice may both represent and maintain the inward unity which should exist in our hearts.

4. Now this uniformity will doubtless be more easily and more perfectly observed if everything that ought to be done be committed to writing, that all may know by means of what is written, how they ought to live ; no one being permitted to alter, to add, or to take away anything according to her own will, lest by neglecting small things, we fall away little by little.

5. In order to provide the better for the unity and peace of the Sisters, we have written this book, which is called the Constitutions, and for the sake of its more convenient use we have divided it in chapters.

SECTION II.

6. OF THE INSTITUTION AND CHARACTER OF THE ORDER AND OF THIS CONGREGATION.

7. As the Order of St. Dominic has been instituted mainly for the salvation of souls, all its members ought to aim at this end by means

suitable to their state. Thus as the Fathers of the Order devote themselves to the office of preaching, for which, as its name implies, the Order was expressly instituted, so the religious women of our Congregation who follow the same holy Rule, should aim at advancing the salvation of souls, both by their prayers and by such active works of charity as may be embraced by their particular Institute. We read that in the very beginning of our Order, our Holy Father St. Dominic founded his first Convent of Nuns at Prouille in France, for the instruction of young girls exposed to the danger of heresy; whence we gather that it entered into the original design of our Holy Patriarch, that the religious women of his Order should occupy themselves with the instruction of others in the faith, when this might be required by the necessities of time and place. In this spirit, therefore, we have embraced the work of teaching.

8. It is most necessary that those who devote themselves to a work so sublime and holy should before all things labor at their own sanctification, that so they may become fit instruments for the sanctification of others,

There are various means by which Religious persons may prepare themselves to work for the salvation of souls, as appears evident from the variety of Religious Institutes approved by the Church, which propose to themselves this end. The means ordained by our Holy Father St. Dominic, and by our venerable ancient Fathers are regular life, monastic observances, and the choral recitation of the Office.

SECTION III.

9. OF THE OBLIGATIONS OF THESE CONSTITUTIONS AND OF DISPENSATIONS.

10. We declare that the Constitutions do not oblige the Sisters under sin, but only under the penalty imposed for their infraction; which penalty if they refuse to accept, they will not escape sin. For as St. Thomas teaches, in our Order the transgression or omission of any point of the Rule or Constitutions, does not of itself bind under sin whether mortal or venial, but only under the assigned penalty, since it is in this manner we are bound to observe them. And although a penalty ought not to be in-

flicted against his will, on one who has committed no sin, yet it may be done in our Order because we have voluntarily bound ourselves to this at our profession.

11. Nevertheless sin may indirectly accompany the transgression: first, when the motive of an action is bad in itself.

12. Secondly, sin is incurred when the transgression of the law is accompanied by formal contempt of the Constitutions, of the Rule or of the Superior.

13. Thirdly, there is sin when the act committed is contrary to the laws of God or of the Church.

14. Fourthly, there is sin when the act committed is against one of the three vows of religion, namely; Poverty, Chastity, or Obedience.

15. In the fifth place, there is sin, when, to the Constitutions is joined the formal precept; —that is, an absolute command made by a lawful Superior, in virtue of the Vow of Obedience.

16. The Prioress shall have power to dispense the Sisters from time to time when she shall judge it to be necessary, excepting on points which the Ecclesiastical Superior or the

Mother-General shall for some reason have reserved to themselves; and such dispensation may be given, not only on account of sickness or infirmity, but also in other cases, when it shall seem good to Superiors, in order not to hinder the greater good of the Order.

17. Nevertheless, the power of dispensation has certain limits. Thus, the grant of some dispensations is reserved to higher Superiors; for a Conventual Prioress cannot grant dispensations from fasting and abstinence to the whole community in a body; although it may happen in a small community, that all the Sisters may have to be individually dispensed, owing to the particular needs of each one, and such a dispensation the Conventual Prioress can legitimately grant. But in this case it would be her duty to inform the Mother-General of it, and to explain the causes.

18. Every Prioress has power in her own Convent, but not in another, to give the necessary dispensations, not only to Sisters of her own community, but also to those of other communities who may be in the same house.

19. The Prioress must not grant any dispensation without just cause. For St. Bernard, in

his book on dispensation, says : " Let not the
Superior add to my vow without my consent,
nor take from it without a certain necessity ;
for the relaxation of the vow without necessity
is not a dispensation, but a dissipation."

But, in order for the Prioress to have a
legitimate motive, it is not necessary that there
be impossibility of keeping the law ; it is sufficient that there be a reasonable cause for the
dispensation. Thus a Prioress may dispense
from the fasts of the Order, not only a Sister
who is ill, but also a Sister who has hard work
to do, or who is in delicate health, or is still
very young ; provided the dispensation do not
exceed the just proportion of the cause which
gave rise to it, and that it do not pass into an
habitual Rule in the Convent.

20. When the Prioress desires a Sister in
her Convent to accept a dispensation, that
Sister must not be too ready to judge that the
Prioress has not a reasonable cause ; for perhaps it is done to humble her, or for some reason of which she is ignorant, as for example :
because there is doubt whether she be not
weak, though the Sister may seem to herself to
be strong. And in this she ought to submit

her judgment to the judgment of her Superior and obey; for it often happens that others can judge better of the weakness of a person from her appearance than can the sufferer herself. Therefore, in doubtful cases, a subject is bound to obey her Superior; obedience in such a case being a sufficient reason.

21. The Sisters cannot dispense themselves, even when there is a just cause, but must have recourse to their Prioress. Superiors, however, may make use of dispensations for themselves when they shall judge it to be expedient, without its being necessary for them to have recourse to higher Superiors.

22. The Prioress cannot dispense the Sisters from the observance of the precepts of the Church, for example, from the fast of Lent, but must apply to the Confessor, not having herself the necessary jurisdiction.

23. When the Prioress is present in the house, the Sub-Prioress, Vicaress and other officials of the Convent shall have no power of dispensation. Nevertheless, the Prioress shall grant to these Sisters such powers as are necessary or useful for the due discharge of their office.

SECTION IV.

24. OF CUSTOMS.

25. Let the laudable ancient customs of our Congregation be kept up; but on the other hand let not customs which are less laudable be introduced; and where they already exist, let them, as far as possible, be abolished.

26. Conventual Prioresses should be diligently on their guard to make no change in approved customs, without the sanction of the Mother-General. And it belongs to the Mother-General in her visitation of the Convents, to correct all those Superiors who introduce abuses or who tolerate in their Convents customs contrary to the laws or regulations of the Congregation, or subversive of religious discipline.

27. Moreover, no Convent shall be accepted in which new customs contrary to the laws and spirit of our Congregation are required to be observed.

28. The Sisters cannot be exempted from the observance of the Constitutions or Ordin-

ances by reason of any custom contrary to them, however long such a custom may have prevailed. Whenever, therefore, a Superior shall require exact observance from any of her subjects they are bound simply to obey, according to the tenor of the protestation made at Profession.

END OF THE PROLOGUE.

PART FIRST.

WHICH TREATS OF THE FORM OF OUR COMMUNITY LIFE AND THE MANNER OF RECEPTION INTO THE CONGREGATION

CHAPTER I.

29. OF THE OFFICE AND OTHER SPIRITUAL EXERCISES

SECTION I.

30. OF PROMPTITUDE IN GOING TO OFFICE.

31. The bell should be rung twice for Office. The first signal should be given by a few strokes only, on hearing which the Sisters must begin to prepare by leaving off the occupations in which they are engaged, and not beginning

new ones. For the second signal the bell should be rung long enough to allow the Sisters who are in the most distant parts of the house to go thence to the Choir. There should be a sufficient interval between the two signals to give the Sisters time for recollection, that they may recite the Office with more devotion.

SECTION II.

32. IN WHAT THE DAILY OFFICE CONSISTS.

33. The Sisters shall recite every day, either in or out of Choir, the Daily Office of the Blessed Virgin, according to the Rite of the Dominican Order, with the commemoration of the Saints of the Order. Moreover, they must say the Office of the Dead every week, the octaves of Easter and Pentecost alone excepted. And those Sisters who are dispensed from the recital of the Office for whatever cause, shall say for Matins 7 Paters and Aves; for Lauds 3: the same, that is, 3 Paters and Aves for each hour, Prime, Terce, Sext and None: for Vespers, 5, and 3 for Compline. ·

34. Those Sisters who say Office out of

Choir are not bound to say in private the Litany of the Blessed Virgin and the *Inviolata* which are sung on Saturdays, nor the Seven Penitential Psalms which are said before Mass on Ash-Wednesday and Maundy-Thursday.

35. According to the universal custom of the Church, let the prayers *Aperi Domine* and *Sacrosanctæ* be said before and after the Office.

36. The custom of singing the Antiphon *Salve Regina* processionally after Compline had its origin with our Holy Father St. Domnic. It was confirmed at Paris in 1226, under the Blessed Jordan. At this procession all the Sisters, even those who are in any way exempted from attendance in Choir, ought to be present, both out of devotion to the Most Holy Mother of God, the especial advocate of our Order, and on account of the 200 days' indulgence which were granted by Paul V. to all persons who shall be present when this Antiphon is sung. At the end of the Salve shall be added the Antiphon *O Lumen* in honor of our Holy Father St. Dominic.

37. Every Saturday the Litany of the Blessed Virgin shall be sung after the *Salve Regina*, as was thus ordained at Bologna in 1615. "On

account of the singular devotion of our Order toward the Blessed Virgin, its especial Patroness, and that we may return some thanks for the innumerable benefits which we have received from her virginal hands, and that she may, especially in these calamitous times, continue her protection to our Order, which sprang up at first through her singular favor and patronage, we will and ordain that, in all the Convents, places and houses of our Order, and in the Monasteries of nuns, the Litany of the Virgin Mother of God be sung every Saturday after the *Salve Regina*, as is already practiced in many Convents of our Order;" and at the end of the Litany, the prose *Inviolata* is to be added as found in the Processional of the Order.

SECTION III.

38. OF THE OBLIGATION OF THE DAILY OFFICE.

39. The Community shall keep Choir according to the Constitutions of the Order, if there are in the house three Sisters capable of reciting the Office, who are not prevented from attendance.

40. All the Professed Sisters are by Rule bound to say the Office. Should they neglect that duty, they would lose the merit of that pious exercise, and render themselves guilty of a trespass of the Constitutions and deserving of correction. The Prioress cannot dispense any Sister from saying Office, unless sickness or some extraordinary occupation render it very difficult to recite it. When a Sister, from any cause whatever, cannot say the Office or any part of the same with the Community, she is bound to say it by herself as soon as she can find an opportunity.

SECTION IV.

41. OF THE MANNER OF RECITING THE OFFICE AND OF THE ATTENTION REQUIRED.

42. In order the more to follow the spirit of the Church in the recitation of the Office, the Sisters shall say Office together in the Convent Chapel. They shall divide themselves equally according to number, so as to have one-half on either side of the Choir, and recite the psalms alternately, in a clear, audible,

slow and pious manner. While thus saying the Office, they shall meditate on the spiritual meaning of the psalms; or, at least, keeping away all worldly thoughts, fix their hearts and minds on God alone.

43. When a Sister says the Office in private, she must recite it so that if she be not deaf, and no obstacle intervene, she can hear her own voice. The Office should be said distinctly, attentively, and with proper reverence, out of Choir as well as in Choir.

SECTION V.

44. OF MENTAL PRAYER.

45. The Sisters must devote themselves to mental prayer in Choir twice every day; that is, for half an hour in the morning and for at least a quarter of an hour in the evening.

When the work of a Convent and its Horarium will admit of it, the evening meditation shall be for half an hour. But when this is the case, on days when the Rosary is said in common, or when Benediction of the Blessed Sacrament is given, these devotions may be reckoned as taking the place of one quarter of an hour of the evening meditation.

46. At these hours of meditation, all the Community ought to be present, except the sick, or those who are in attendance on them, or whose offices oblige them at such times to be absent from Choir. But if from these or other causes a Sister be sometimes absent from Choir at the time of meditation, she is nevertheless bound on the same day to devote herself to mental prayer for at least the space of half an hour. Those only are excepted who are on a journey, or who are really prevented by illness, or who are in close attendance on the sick.

47. It is strictly forbidden to Superiors to shorten, and yet more entirely to omit, the time of common meditation, unless for some urgent necessity. Prioresses should be most vigilant that all the religious who are present at the meditation shall remain in Choir to the end. Nor must they allow the requirements of any office to interfere with this important duty beyond what is of strict necessity. And the Mother-General, at her visitations, must inquire with particular care into the observance of this

point of the Constitutions. At the beginning of the Meditation a passage should be read aloud from some spiritual author.

48. Let the Sisters be mindful of that which the Apostle says in his First Epistle to Timothy : " Bodily exercise is profitable to little." For we profit more by the exercise of pious affections toward God than is possible for us by the service of the lips only. Hence spiritual writers warn us that they are mistaken who set themselves a daily task of vocal prayer in preference to meditation and mental prayer, for this would be to neglect the end for the means. And Saint Bonaventure says : " The Religious who does not assiduously give himself to prayer, is not only wretched and useless, but in the eyes of God, he carries a dead soul in a living body. Nor is it wonderful if he who is not zealous and constant in prayer, should often miserably yield to temptation." Let all Prioresses, therefore, see that this holy practice is observed in their Convents, remembering that mental prayer conduces to excite and maintain the fire of divine love in the soul, according to the words of the Royal Prophet : " In my meditation a fire shall flame out."

SECTION VI.

49. OF SPIRITUAL READING.

50. The duty and importance of Spiritual Reading as one of the daily exercises of a Religious, are sufficiently indicated by Saint Augustine in the Rule where he says that the books may be asked for at a certain hour every day. Every Sister, therefore, should endeavor to make Spiritual Reading when her other duties permit, for at least a quarter of an hour every day.

SECTION VII.

51. OF THE ANNUAL SPIRITUAL RETREAT.

52. All the Sisters without exception, are bound to make a spiritual retreat every year for the space of eight days, though they are not bound all to make it at the same time, or to have a preached retreat. It is permitted by custom to reckon as eight days, six full days, adding part of the evening on which the retreat begins, and part of the morning of

the eighth day on which it ends. The practice
of the annual retreat is very useful for shaking
off the dust of worldly things, which cannot
help attaching itself to the hearts even of religious persons, amidst the manifold solicitudes
of life. Moreover, many Sovereign Pontiffs
have granted indulgences for the performance
of these exercises.

SECTION VIII.

**53. OF THE CONFRATERNITIES OF THE HOLY
ROSARY, OF THE HOLY NAME AND OF THE
ANGELIC WARFARE.**

54. In common with all the children of St.
Dominic we are bound to cherish a great love
for the most salutary devotion of the Holy Rosary, which was bequeathed to us as a special
birthright by our Holy Father, has been used
ever since as a most powerful weapon in the
spiritual warfare by all the Saints of our Order,
and has been enriched by many Sovereign Pontiffs with a vast treasure of indulgences. Following out the spirit of our Institute, we also
are bound, no less than the Fathers, to attach

ourselves to this devotion in preference to all others, and to spare no pains that its use shall be constantly taught and explained to the children of our schools and to all under our care.

55. All the Brethren and Sisters of the Order, from the time of making their profession are members of the Confraternity of the Rosary, so that it is not necessary for them to be enrolled in the Book of the Confraternity.

56. To gain the Indulgences attached to the Confraternity it is requisite to say the whole Rosary once during the week; but it is not necessary to say more than a third part at a time. Although this suffice to fulfil the strict obligation of the Confraternity, yet every Sister ought to recite at least one third part of the Rosary daily, either privately or in common, as a devotion second only in importance to the Office and Meditation prescribed by the Constitution. Let us therefore rejoice in the possession of so great a treasure, and as true children of our Holy Father, greatly love the Holy Rosary, assiduously use it and zealously propagate it, according to the means proper to our state; being assured that the blessing of God would cease to rest on our Congregation

should we ever come to neglect this precious devotion whose perfume was shed around the very cradle of our Holy Order.

57. The Confraternity of the Holy Name of God, or of Jesus, was instituted in the first century of the Order for the purpose of extirpating the vice of blasphemy, and to lead men to worship and reverence that Most Holy Name with due religious honor. This Confraternity, already recommended by several General Chapters, has been still more earnestly pressed upon us in our own day by the Master of the Order, Father Brother Alexander Vincent Jandel. The Brethren and Sisters of the Order cannot gain the indulgences with which this Confraternity has been enriched by the Holy See, unless their names be duly enrolled in the Book of the Confraternity. The principal Feast of this Confraternity is on the first of January.

58. The Roman Pontiffs have also granted many favors to the Confraternity of the Angelic Warfare, or Girdle of Saint Thomas Aquinas. In order to gain them, it is necessary to be inscribed in the Book of the Confraternity, and to wear day and night around the waist, the girdle blessed by a Priest of the Order, or by

some other Priest having faculties from the Master-General.

The fifteen Hail Maries said on the cord of Saint Thomas should be recited in honor of the fifteen Mysteries of the Rosary, and are a kind of abridgment of that devotion. An indulgence of sixty days is attached to their recitation.

The principal Feast of this Confraternity is January 28th, being that of the Translation of the relics of the Holy Doctor.

SECTION IX.

59. OF VARIOUS ORDINANCES RELATING TO THIS CHAPTER.

60. The Mother-General, as well as each Conventual Prioress, must bestow all care and diligence on the adornment and beauty of the Chapels attached to our Convents, especially in those things which are used for the celebration of Mass and the administration of the Holy Eucharist. Let Superiors, therefore, remove such Sacristans as are negligent in the duties of their office. For, as was declared at the Chapter of Rome (A. D. 1756): the very na-

ture of our Holy Order requires that we should love and have a care for the beauty of God's house.

61. All the Altars in the Churches of the Order are privileged for the Priests of the Order celebrating at them, in suffrage for the souls of all the faithful departed; and this holds good, even if the Masses be not of the Dead, whether they be of obligation or devotion. The Altars in our houses and in possessions belonging to us are also privileged.

62. Altar stones must be neatly let into the middle of the table of the Altar, so as to rise somewhat above the level of the Altar, and to be easily discernible by the touch.

63. The table of the Altar, especially if it be a consecrated Altar, must be clean and decently ornamented. It must be covered by three linen cloths, blessed by a Bishop, or by some one having that power. The uppermost of these cloths, at least, must be long enough to reach to the ground; the other two may be shorter, or one may be used doubled. There should be also a proper Altar covering, that the linen cloths may be preserved from dust and other impurities.

64. In every house of our Institute, whether Priory or Vicariate, let Altars be erected in the Dormitories in honor of the Blessed Virgin, our most compassionate Advocate and Mistress.

65. In the Sacristy a tablet shall be hung up on which shall be inscribed the anniversaries which the Convent observes.

66. The corporals shall be two palms in width and two palms and a half, at least, in length, of plain white cloth made of unmixed linen; they shall not be embroidered or interwoven with silk.

The cruets shall not be made of anything but glass, and that not colored, but clear, with metal lids.

CHAPTER II.

SECTION I.

68. OF THE INCLINATIONS IN GENERAL.

69. We distinguish three kinds of inclinations, two kinds of genuflections, and two of prostrations.

70. The three kinds of inclinations are: First, the profound inclination, which is made by bending the head and body in such a manner that the elbows may rest upon the knees; secondly, the middle inclination, which is made by bending the head and body so that the hands can touch the knees; and thirdly, the inclination of the head, which is made by merely slightly bending the head and body.

71. The two kinds of genuflections are: The genuflection on both knees, which simply consists in kneeling on both knees, keeping

the body erect, and the genuflection on one knee.

72. The two kinds of prostrations are: First the prostration properly so called, which is made by kneeling and leaning forward with the elbows and body over the benches, or upon the knees when there are no benches; and the prostration called *Venia;* this is made by extending the whole body on the ground lying on the right side, keeping one leg upon the other.

73. Moreover, the Sisters may stand or sit; they may turn toward the Altar, or face Choir to Choir.

SECTION II.

74. HOW THE MOST HOLY SACRAMENT IS TO BE ADORED ON ENTERING THE CHOIR, AND OF THE CEREMONIES OF THE OFFICE.

75. When the Sisters come into Choir for Office, or present themselves before the Most Holy Sacrament of the Eucharist, though it be only in passing before the Altar, they shall make the profound inclination, and also the genuflection on one knee, on account of the

majesty of God, and the real Presence of the
Most Holy Body of our Lord Jesus Christ.

76. At the signal given by the Superioress,
the Sisters standing and turned toward the
Altar, shall say the first part of the *Ave Maria.*
The hour being thus devoutly begun :

They shall turn toward the Altar during the
Deus in adjutorium, etc., making the sign of
the cross ; but at the *Gloria Patri* they shall
bow profoundly, facing Choir to Choir until the
Sicut erat.   At the Invitatory the Sisters stand
processionally, except at the words *Venite
adoremus*, when they kneel, facing Choir to
Choir; this is done also at that verse of the *Te
Deum, Te ergo quæsumus.*   At the *Gloria Patri*
at the end of the Invitatory, they bow to the
knees, and then remain facing Choir to Choir
until the end of the Office.   At the first Psalm,
one Choir shall sit and the other stand.   At
the second Psalm, the Choir which had been
seated rises and the other sits down, and so on
alternately until the *Laudate Dominum* of
Lauds, when all must be either standing or inclined until the end of the Hour.

The same order is to be observed at all the
Hours of the Office.   Both Choirs sit after the

blessing, while the Lessons at Matins are read, and during the Responsories. The profound inclination is made at the *Pater*, before the lessons; but the middle inclination is made throughout the Office, whenever the holy Names of Jesus and Mary are said in the Prayers, during the last verse of the Hymns, the last verse but one of the canticle *Benedicite*, and the *Gloria Patri* at the end of each Psalm.

SECTION III.

77. OF THE THREE KINDS OF INCLINATIONS.

78 The profound inclination is made: At the first *Gloria Patri* of each hour; when the *Pater* is said in Choir, at Grace, Vespers and Matins of the Office of the Dead, and in the Chapter. On Sundays and Festivals, during the first Collect of the Mass when it is sung, at the prayer for the Church, at the Post Communion, and at these words: *Per Dominum nostrum Jesum Christum*, which end the last Prayer of the Mass and Office.

79. The middle inclination is made: 1st. At every *Gloria Patri*, except the first at each

hour, the Sisters rising at the *Sicut erat.* 2d. During the Blessings given, either in Choir or before meals. 3d. At the words in the *Gloria in excelsis: Gratias agimus tibi propter magnam gloriam tuam;* also at those, *Suscipe deprecationem nostram.* 4th. During those words of the preface : *Gratias agamus Domino Deo nostro.* 5th. Every time the most holy Names of Jesus and Mary are pronounced in the Prayers at Mass, in the Preface, and in the antiphon *Salve,* in the *Gloria in excelsis,* and at the names of our Blessed Father Saint Dominic, and our Seraphic Mother Saint Catharine, in the Prayers. 6th. During the last verse of the Hymn, and the last verse but one of the canticle *Benedicite.*

80. The inclination of the head is made: 1st. When we pronounce the most holy Names of Jesus and Mary, or of Saint Dominic or Saint Catharine in any other place, except in the Prayers. 2d. After a Sister has intoned a Psalm or said a Capitulum, or Versicle, or anything else. 3d. When the words *Sit nomen Domine Benedictum* occur. 4th. At the words in the Creed *Qui cum Patre et Filio simul adoratur, et conglorificatur.* 5th. At every *Gloria*

Patri when the office is said in private. 6th. When holy water is given, as at the *Asperges*, or the *Vidi Aquam* on Sunday, or during the chant of the *Salve.* 7th. On receiving any article of clothing or anything else, saying at the same time, *Benedictus Deus in donis suis,* or " *Blessed be God in all His gifts.*" 8th. When the Prioress tells a Sister to do or say anything, and when a Superior enjoins any order on all the Community. 9th. The head should be bent with respect when passing Superiors.

81. Any exceptions to certain inclinations, will be explained in the Book of Customs.

SECTION IV.

82. OF THE TWO KINDS OF GENUFLECTIONS.

83. The genuflection on one knee, as we have said, is to be made on coming into the presence of the Blessed Sacrament; and the genuflection on both knees, besides what has been already said for the Office, is to be made during the first verse of the *Ave Maris stella*, at Vespers, and at any other time; when the anthem *Sub tuum* is said in Choir; at the first

words of the *Salve Regina* at Compline, and from the words *Eia ergo* in the *Salve* to *O Clemens,* during which all kneel turned toward the Altar. When the *Salve Sancta Parens* is sung in Choir ; at the words of the Gospel for Epiphany, *Et procidentes adoraverunt eum ;* at the words *Adjuva nos Deus salutaris noster,* in the Masses in Lent ; at the words *Ave Rex,* sung in the procession on Palm Sunday ; at the verse *Tantum Ergo* of the hymn *Pange lingua ;* at the first verse of the *Veni Creator ;* at the words *Et incarnatus est de Spiritu Sancto,* in the Credo of the Mass ; at the verse of the Hymn of the Passion, *O Crux ave, Spes unica,* to do homage to the Passion of our Lord, and when the words *Domine, miserere super peccatrice,* are sung at the Office of Burial of the Sisters ; during the *Salve Regina* and prayers which are said after the Hours of the Office ; during the Litany of the Blessed Virgin and the *Inviolata,* said or sung on Saturday after Compline. The genuflection on both knees is made also whenever the Priest says *Flectamus genua ;* at the Adoration of the Cross on Good Friday ; each time the Choir sings *Sanctus Deus ;* whenever we enter or leave the presence of the Blessed Sacrament when exposed, bowing the head at the same time; during the elevation of the Most Holy Body and Blood of Jesus Christ in the Mass, except when the prostration is made.

SECTION V.

84. OF THE TWO KINDS OF PROSTRATIONS.

85. The first kind of prostration, that is to say, the prostration over the benches, is to be made, besides the occasions mentioned above:

1st. On all Sundays and Festivals, from after the Elevation until the *Pater* exclusively.

2d. At all masses of the Feria, from the *Sanctus* to the *Agnus Dei* exclusively. During the Paschal season the prostration is made only from the Elevation to the *Pater*.

3d. At the first Prayer of the Mass, the Prayer for the Church, at the first Post Communion, and at the words *Per Dominum nostrum Jesum Christum Filium Tuum*, which end the last prayer of the Mass.

4th. During the Absolution of Faults.

5th. On Ash Wednesday and Holy Thursday, when the Penitential Psalms are said before Mass.

6th. On Good Friday, when the priest sings *Ecce Lignum Crucis* and *Super omnia.*

7th. At the words *Veneremur cernui* of the verse *Tantum ergo.*

8th. When the Blessed Sacrament is being moved; whilst the Priest gives Holy Communion, and at the Blessing at Benediction.

9th. When in the singing of the Passion, the words *Emisit Spiritum* are pronounced.

86. The second prostration called *Venia*, is made:

1st. After the Office, when any notable fault has been committed, either in reading or singing amiss, and the Sister remains prostrate until the Superioress gives her the signal to rise. The same is to be done in the Refectory when a Sister has committed any fault in reading, or eating, or serving at table.

2d. At the Chapter of faults, when the Prioress says, *Let those who are guilty make the prostration*, and also after each Sister has said her faults.

3d. When a formal precept is given, obligatory on those present.

4th. When any Sister has offended or scandalized another, the *Venia* is then made at the feet of the sister offended.

SECTION VI.

87. OF THE TIMES WHEN THE SISTERS STAND FACING THE ALTAR, WHEN THEY STAND FACING CHOIR TO CHOIR, AND WHEN THEY SIT DOWN.

88. The Sisters stand facing Choir to Choir:

1st. During the Office as is marked above.

2d. At the High Mass, as indicated in the ceremonial. They turn toward the altar when the priest sings, or responses have to be made; but if a middle or a profound inclination has to be made, they turn chorally. They sit—

1st. From the beginning of the Vespers of the Dead until the *Magnificat.*

2d. During the Epistle and during the Prophecies on Good Friday and Holy Saturday, and at other times marked in the Ceremonial.

3d. At Matins of the Dead from the beginning until *Laudate Dominum de coelis*, exclusively; except at the *Pater noster* said before

the Lessons, during which the profound incli-
nation is made. But at the last response of
Matins, at the words *Creator omnium rerum
Deus*, all should stand.

89. The prostrations and genuflections prescribed by the Constitutions shall never be
made in public and are obligatory only in
Choir, not on Sisters reciting the Office in
private. In whatever place the Community is
assembled out of Choir, whether in the Refectory or the Chapter Room, for Grace or other
similar prayers, inclinations are always to be
made instead of prostrations. The Sisters who
are reciting or singing a versicle which the
Choir is inclined, should make the inclination
at the close of the versicle.

The other occasions on which the inclinations, genuflections and prostrations mentioned
above are to be made, are indicated in the
Ceremonial and in other Liturgical books.

CHAPTER III.

90. OF THE SUFFRAGES FOR THE DEAD.

91. Between the Feast of Saint Dionysius (October 9), and the First Sunday of Advent, every Sister shall say the Psalter, and those in any way dispensed from the Choir, shall say one hundred and fifty *Pater nosters*, and one hundred and fifty *Ave Marias* for the anniversary of the Brethren and Sisters, and of those who have been received by letter to the benefits of the Order. The same must be said by every Sister when any Sister of the Congregation dies, and in each Convent a Mass shall be offered for the repose of her soul. The same suffrages must be said by every Sister of the Congregation for the Ecclesiastical Superior, and for the Master-General or Vicar-General of the Order at their decease.

92. Each Sister shall also say the seven Penitential Psalms thirty times a year for our Brethren and Sisters departed, and those in any

way dispensed from Choir shall say thirty times twenty-five *Pater nosters* and *Ave Marias.*

93. Four anniversaries shall be kept in the year:

1st. The anniversary of the Fathers and Mothers, which shall be on the third day after the Feast of the Purification of the Blessed Virgin (February 4).

2d. The Anniversary of our Benefactors and Familiars, which shall be the next day after the Octave of Saint Augustine (September 5).

3d. The Anniversary of all who are buried in our Cemeteries, which shall be kept everywhere on July 12.

4th. The Anniversary of the Brethren and Sisters, which shall be kept on November 10.

94. The death of any Sister should be announced as soon as possible to all those who are bound to offer prayers on her behalf, in order that the deceased may be speedily assisted by the suffrages of the living.

95. The Mother General shall cause to be inscribed in the Acts of every General Chapter of the Congregation, the names of those Sisters who have departed this life since the preceding Chapter. And let her take care to have added

a short account of the life and actions of each Sister, and especially of those who have been remarkable for their virtues.

96. In the Convent where a Sister dies or is buried, let a *Requiem* Mass be celebrated, and let the whole Office of the Dead be said for her soul, even if the .whole or part of it has already been said. But if the Office has not yet been recited, that which is said for the departed Sister suffices for the obligation of that week. At this Office the highest Superior present in the house should preside. A *Requiem* Mass must also be celebrated for her in every Convent of the Congregation on receiving the news of her death, when this can be done; but if this cannot be done, the Mass of the day should be said for the repose of her soul. The other prayers to be recited beside the body of the deceased are prescribed in the Ceremonial. Whatever is done for a deceased Sister before burial shall be over and above that which is due to her in virtue of the Constitutions, that is to say, in the Convent where she dies; for in other Convents of the Congregation the suffrages may be begun immediately on hearing the news of her death.

97. For eight days after the burial of any Religious of the Community, the Sisters shall say the Response *Libera me Domine*, when they have finished the Grace after dinner.

98. On hearing of the death of the Master-General or Vicar-General of the Order, let a solemn Mass be celebrated where this can suitably be done, and let the Office of the Dead be recited in every Convent of the Congregation in the manner explained above. The same should be done on hearing of the death of the Vicar of the General, or of the Mother General or of an ex-Mother General. The suffrages which are appointed for the Master of the Order are due to him even if he dies being no longer General: but this is not the case with regard to the Ecclesiastical Superior.

99. The Psalm *De Profundis* shall be recited outside the Refectory before dinner and supper for our deceased benefactors.

100. The Sisters are to be buried in the complete religious habit, with the face covered.

CHAPTER IV.

101. OF CONFESSION, OF MASS AND HOLY COMMUNION.

SECTION I.

102. OF CONFESSION.

103. The Sisters are bound to go to Confession frequently, and as a rule once a week, even if it should so happen that they are not going to Communion.

104. The Church of God, always careful to preserve liberty of conscience, from time to time granted to religious Communities an extraordinary Confessor. It will, then, be a rule never to be dispensed with, to ask the Bishop for a Confessor, besides the ordinary one, two or three times a year, at the time which shall seem most opportune. The Sisters are not bound to make their Confession to him, but for the sake of regularity and humility, all shall present themselves at the Confessional. Should the Pri-

oress know that any Sister is anxious to confess out of the regular time, or to another Confessor, she shall not refuse her request, if it can
easily be granted.

SECTION II.

105. OF MASS AND HOLY COMMUNION.

106. When the Sisters cannot have a Chapel
on their own premises, or when they cannot
have Mass celebrated in it, they are bound to
go to the Church to attend Divine Service
every Sunday and Festival of obligation.

107. Let the Sisters avoid speaking in the
Church, except from actual necessity, and then
only in a subdued tone; and let them be particularly careful not to speak at the Church
doors or in the porch, or carry on unnecessary
conversations in the vestry.

108. The Sisters shall make a general Com-
munion every Sunday in the year, and on the
Feasts of Christmas, Circumcision, Epiphany,
Holy Thursday, Easter, Ascension and Corpus
Christi, likewise on all the Feasts of the Blessed
Virgin, on those of All Saints, the Holy

Apostles Peter and Paul, of all Apostles, of St. Joseph, of our Holy Father St. Dominic, and of the Saints of the Order. Let no one stay away from Holy Communion on those days without special leave. The Sisters may communicate on other days with the permission of the Confessor. Those who are out of the Convent must communicate out of the Convent or as soon as they can conveniently after their return. When several communicating days immediately succeed each other, the Sisters may be dispensed on some of them.

109. The mantles must always be worn at Holy Communion.

CHAPTER V.

110. OF FASTING AND ABSTINENCE.

111. Although it may be very laudable to conform to the Constitutions of the Third Order in regard to the Fasts, nevertheless, taking into consideration the occupations of the Schools, and the labors of the Sisters of this Institute, they shall be obliged to observe only the Fasts of the Church, and on every Friday of the year.

112. On Good Friday the Sisters may, if they are able, fast on bread and water.

113. As a token of the great reverence and devotion, which we desire to cherish towards our Holy Father St. Dominic, let the eve of his Feast be observed as a fast. If the Feast should fall on Monday, the fast must be kept on the previous Saturday. But this fast on the eve of our Holy Father St. Dominic being an obligation voluntarily assumed by the Congregation from the Constitutions of the Great Order, must not be considered so strictly bind-

ing as the fast on Fridays, which is enjoined by the Rule of the Third Order.

114. On fasting days, Superiors ought to provide their subjects with extra food in the Refectory, that they may be better able to fast.

115. Those who are on a journey are bound to observe the fasts which are commonly observed in the country where they are.

116. If there be any Sisters who, without any cause, habitually break the fasts of the Order, and are in the disposition to persevere in that transgression, such Sisters would be in danger of falling into that contempt which is not without sin.

CHAPTER VI.

117. OF THE REFECTORY.

SECTION I.

118. OF THE MEALS AND MANNER OF SERVING AT TABLE.

119. At a convenient time before dinner and supper the Sacristan shall ring a few strokes on the great bell, that the Sisters may not delay in coming to the Refectory. Then, if the meal be ready, the bell shall be rung, but it shall not be rung until all is ready.

120. When the bell is rung for meals, the Sisters must go promptly and in silence to the place where they wash their hands. Having washed their hands, the Superioress shall begin the *De Profundis*, and shall say one verse herself, the others all answering and saying the next verse, and at the end shall be said the Prayer *Fidelium*. Then the Prioress shall

ring the little bell of the Refectory, and the Sisters shall enter two and two, the youngest first; and on reaching the middle of the Refectory, they shall reverently bow before the Cross, or the Image, which is placed above the seat of the Prioress, and shall arrange themselves on each side, and the Community shall proceed with the blessing of the table. This being ended, the Sisters shall seat themselves at table, but no one shall begin to eat till the Reader has read two sentences. They shall take their food in silence during the reading, and shall not over-much prolong the meal.

121. With regard to serving at table, it has been ordained that in handing the dishes the Servers shall always begin at the lower tables and so go up to the table of the Prioress, unless the Prioress should order otherwise, when more than two Servers are necessary. But in taking away the plates, and the remains of the meal, they shall begin with the Prioress' table and go down thence to the lower tables.

122. At the end of the meal the Superioress having given the signal with the little bell, the Reader shall conclude her reading with these words: "Tu autem, Domine, miserere nostri,"

or, But Thou, O Lord, have mercy on us: and the Sisters shall answer: "Deo gratias," or, Thanks be to God. After this the Prioress shall ring the little bell until the Sisters have risen from the table. When the bell has ceased ringing, those who have committed any fault in serving, eating or reading shall make their *venia*, and at a signal from the Prioress they shall return to their places. Then the Sisters shall say Grace.

123. When any one perceives that the one next her wants anything, she shall ask the Server for it. But no Sister except the Prioress may send any portion of food to another Sister, though every Sister may give a part of what has been set before her, to those only who are seated next her, on the right hand or on the left.

124. Let nothing special be served to any Sister at table that is not given to the rest of the Community, whatever rank or office she may hold, except by reason of sickness or infirmity, and with leave.

125. The Prioress shall eat in the Refectory, and shall be content with the ordinary food of the Community; so also shall the Infirmarians and the other Sisters who are engaged in any

office whatever, unless the Prioress shall give dispensation, to some, for a good reason, to eat elsewhere.

126. No Sister shall be absent from the first table, unless with leave, and for some cause. Those that have been absent from the first table shall come to the second table, so that it shall not be necessary to have a third.

127. All notable superfluities in food and drink, on occasion of General Chapters, are prohibited, as also all expensive entertainments on occasions of Clothings and Professions.

128. Seculars must never be permitted to eat in the Refectory.

129. It is forbidden to eat in the cells, unless in case of sickness or with special leave, and the Cellarer is forbidden to furnish anything to those who wish to eat apart from the common table, without leave, and without necessity.

. 130. The *Laudate Dominum omnes gentes*, shall be substituted for the *Miserere* on great Feasts.

SECTION II.

131. OF READING AT TABLE.

132. The public reading shall last during the whole of the meal. For it is written in the Rule of St. Augustine : "When you go to table, listen without noise or contention to that which is read to you according to custom, until you rise from your meal."

133. There should be a Correctress appointed, who should at once rectify the faults which the Reader may make, and direct her, in case selections have to be made out of the volume appointed. In order the better to acquit herself of her Office, the Correctress should look over beforehand what has to be read. She should, if possible, have her seat near the Reader.

134. The Reader, when beginning a new book, should say : " Here begins (name of such a book) ; " if it has been already begun, " Continuation of (name of such a book); " and when she comes to the conclusion, " Here ends (name of such a book)." In reading the Gos-

pel, when she comes to the Passion, she should pass on to the Resurrection.

135. On all days except Sundays, and feasts marked first-class, in the Order, either the Rule of St. Augustine, or part of the Constitutions, shall be read, so that the Rule of St. Augustine be read once a week, and the whole of the Constitutions about once in a year. A copy of the Constitutions shall be kept in the Refectory, marked out in portions for this purpose.

Chapter VII.

136. OF THE WORK.

137. Forasmuch as idleness is the enemy of the soul, and the mother and nurse of all vices, let none of the Sisters be idle, but let this be carefully observed, that except at those hours and times when they are engaged in prayer, in reciting the Office, or in any other necessary employment, they all be diligently occupied, either in some manual labor for the general good, or in study, in order to fit themselves for being useful in the schools, according as shall be appointed them. When the Sisters are assembled for work, let the Prioress, Sub-Prioress, or some other Sister appointed for the purpose, be present. The Sisters shall work in silence, and no Sister may leave the workroom without permission and necessity. Whoever has thus left the room, must return as soon as she has accomplished that for which she left it.

138. Under the name of work, are included various kinds of useful and necessary occupations. First, are to be understood those domestic and laborious offices in the Convent from taking part in which none should be excused, such as the kitchen, laundry, infirmary and the like. Secondly, the active charitable works undertaken by the Sisters of our Congregation. Thirdly, needlework or other manual work done for the common good. The Sisters employed in this last kind of work should meet in the common work-room, unless for special reasons, it be appointed otherwise, or the small number of the Community should render it impossible. The Sisters are not bound, however, to be always in the work-room, but may spend some time in their cells or elsewhere, to work or pray, as the Prioress may appoint, or as may be prescribed in the Customary.

CHAPTER VIII.

139. OF THE SICK.

140. The Prioress shall take care that she be not negligent toward the sick, for the sick should be treated so that they may soon recover, as our Father St. Augustine says in the Rule. They may be allowed to eat meat, as their sickness or weakness may require, according to the judgment of the Prioress.

141. In every Convent there should be a convenient Infirmary for those who are sick or out of health, and one principal Infirmarian should be appointed, with one or more assistants as may be required. The Prioress is bound kindly and frequently to visit the sick Sisters, and to provide for their necessities. Nor is the Cellarer to show herself harsh or unwilling to purchase the medicines, or other remedies, which are needful for the sick, but let her charitably comply with the requests of the Infirmarian, and provide all things according

as the means of the house will allow, even at the sacrifice if necessary, of the goods of the Convent. Prioresses and Syndics who shall be found negligent in this matter shall be deprived of their offices, a penalty which the Mother General shall be careful to enforce.

142. If any Sister should be attacked with a contagious malady, she must be taken care of in some separate place, apart from the rest of the sick.

143. The sick who are not confined to their beds must not speak during the time of deep silence, or during meals.

144. When the Prioress is sick, it belongs to the Sub-Prioress to have due care of her health, and to see that she has the requisite dispensations, referring to the Mother General in case of need. When the Prioress is sick, let her be taken care of with the rest in the Infirmary.

145. In the Infirmary the use of woolen mattresses and of linen sheets is permitted when necessary, and the sick are allowed to wear linen next the skin when some special infirmity requires it.

Chapter IX.

146. OF THE BEDS, THE DORMITORIES, AND THE CELLS.

147. The Sisters shall not sleep on feather-beds, but on straw-beds or mattresses. They shall wear at night, the tunic, veil cap and cincture; the scapular is part of the habit, and must be worn whenever the Sisters appear before others; but it is not necessary to wear it at night though the Sisters should leave it near them, that they may be at all times under the protection of the Blessed Virgin. No Sister shall sleep out of the common Dormitory, except the sick, those who have care of them, and those who have charge of pupils.

148. Each Sister should be content with one cell in the common Dormitory. There must be no superfluous or vain ornaments, nor profane pictures or images, but there may be a Crucifix with a statue of the Blessed Virgin in each cell; also a picture or statue of St. Dom-

inic, and some other pious pictures, as may represent the special devotions of our Order, and
the particular works of our Congregation. But
there must be moderation in the use of these
as becomes Religious, whose lives should be
simple, poor and hidden in God.

CHAPTER X.

149. OF THE HABIT.

150. OF THE HABIT OF THE ORDER.

151. The Habit of the Order is a white tunic, a white Scapular, a white veil for the unprofessed Sisters, a black veil for the Professed Sisters, and a black mantle for all. These habits, except the white veil, shall be of woolen stuff, decent, but not costly, and in particular, the mantles shall be of coarse material. Because wearing the dress too short seems to indicate some levity, and a long dress shows greater decorum and gravity, we are not allowed to wear our habits too short, but they ought to come down within an inch of the ground. The mantle must be shorter than the habit by three inches. The scapular must be somewhat shorter than the habit, neither too narrow nor too wide, but just wide enough to cover the seam that fastens the sleeves into the habit.

Neither the mantle, habit nor scapular ought to drag upon the ground.

152. The mantle is worn at Holy Communion, for solemn processions, and at the Ceremonies of Clothing and Profession. The Sisters should wear the mantle also when assisting at any service in the Church, and when obliged to go out of their Convent.

153. Our clothes ought to be conformable to religious poverty. The clothing of the Sisters must be bought out of the common fund, and must be altogether uniform, both for private Religious and for Superiors, and so conformable to that state of poverty which **we have** professed, that nothing superfluous be allowed on the one hand, and on the other, that nothing necessary be denied to any one.

SECTION II.

154. OF THE OBLIGATION OF SUPERIORS TO SUPPLY THEIR SUBJECTS WITH CLOTHING AND OF THE HABIT ROOM.

155. Prioresses are bound to provide their subjects with sufficient clothing, and especially

tunicles, under pain of absolution from office, if they be found negligent in this matter; lest the Sisters lacking due and ordinary help in their necessities, be led through the negligence of their Superiors, into the vice of appropriation. And this distribution must be made without respect of persons.

156. All the clothes of the Sisters, even if assigned to the use of any individual, as also sheets, towels and all things used in common, must be kept together in some convenient place in the Convent, and there diligently taken care of by one or two Sisters assigned to this office; and according to the orders of the Superior, these shall distribute them to each according to her need, as our Father St. Augustine enjoins in the Rule. If the Sisters receive from their relations clothing, or money with which to buy it, all must be placed at the service of the Community, as prescribed in the Rule of St. Augustine.

157. The hair must be kept close cut, as becomes Religious.

SECTION III.

158. OF THE DRESS OF THE CHILDREN EDUCATED IN OUR CONVENTS.

159. In Convents where girls are received for their education, they should be lodged apart, and if such a place be not yet provided on account of the poverty of the Convent, let it be provided as soon as possible, and let them be under the care of Sisters, appointed their Mistresses, who shall bring them up in a Religious manner. Nothing should be allowed the children, either in their clothing or the furniture of their apartments, which savors of the spirit of the world, but they must be formed to all virtue and modesty such as should reign in Convents and among Religious women, whose minds should be wholly turned away from secular vanities.

CHAPTER XI.

160. OF THE SCHOOLS AND THE OBLIGATIONS OF THE TEACHERS.

SECTION I.

161. OF THE OBLIGATIONS OF THE TEACHERS IN GENERAL.

162. The particular rules which the Sisters must follow in teaching, are detailed in the Customary. • Meanwhile, it is advisable to remind them here of certain general rules which they ought to observe if they wish their ministry to be of profit to themselves and their neighbor.

1st. The Christian education of children being that particular work which God has entrusted to them among all the works practiced in the Church, they ought always to be disposed to perform it courageously, even though certain that the fatiguing labor will, in the end, exhaust their strength. In order to persevere steadily in this devotion and to practice it in the most enlightened manner, they shall make themselves very familiar with the principles of Faith, which can sustain and develop it, as: the great love of our Lord Jesus Christ for man; the dignity of the soul ransomed by His Blood; the import of His divine law; the sanctity of His judgments; the eternity of His penalties and rewards; the virtue of the Sacraments, and the maternal love of Mary for children.

2d. Meanwhile let them remember that they are *Religious above all*, who have made Profession in an Institute approved, and have assumed the obligation of aiming at perfection. It may happen that age, infirmities, duties may relieve them from the charge of children; on the other hand no service performed for one's neighbor can dispense them from laboring for their own sanctification, by the correction of faults and the acquisition of virtues, nor excuse them if they begin to abandon the first of all duties.

3d. But, although perfection exists in the interior of the soul, the Sisters will vainly persuade themselves that they can acquire it by neglecting the exterior exercises of the spiritual life. The Saints themselves, with all their acquired virtues, took long hours from apostolical labors to spend in the affairs of God. A Religious then, cannot without temerity, believe that continuance in exterior activity takes the place of the regular exercises, furnishes her with the means of searching into those matters that relate to perfection, aids her in daily renewing her spirit. This is why among exterior works, Superiors shall take care that each Sister, except in extraordinary cases, may have time to perform all the religious acts which are ordained for her perfection. Superiors shall also take care that there remains at the Mother-House a sufficient number of Sisters to maintain the conventual life in all its regularity and beauty, so that those who return from secondary Houses, may there find the repose, light and joy which they need in order to reanimate their fervor.

4th. Amongst all the religious virtues to which the Sisters should apply themselves incessantly, the spirit of obedience is that one which their occupation renders most indispensable. Without this, while disquieting and fatiguing themselves, they may, perhaps, obtain the approval of the world, and this will be all their recompense, vain as their own souls. With the spirit of obedience, they will submit their works of zeal to the direction of Superiors, voluntarily and simply, and their most humble actions shall be blessed of God.

5th. Moreover, as our Institute has for principal scope, the education of children, the Sisters must not neglect their obligation to fit themselves to the best of their ability for this important work, and for the furtherance of this object, let Superiors take care to provide their subjects who are engaged in teaching, with necessary advantages and sufficient time for study as far as the means of the Convent will ermit.

6th. Finally, considering that they have to do good to people in the world, and that great spiritual gifts may be rendered useless by the manner of using them, they shall take care to practice toward those secular persons whom their labors compel them to meet, that Christian courtesy and that dignified, reserved, upright and humble manner of which our Holy Father St. Dominic has given us the perfect model.   For it is written of him :   " He showed great civility of manner, and as a contented heart gladdens the countenance of man, one could easily judge of his interior peace by the joyousness of his countenance, which no movement of anger ever disturbed.   While his face   shone   with a loving   and   tender light, this brightness never seemed puerile, but easily won   all hearts.   Nothing   was   more natural to him than to rejoice with the happy, to weep with the sorrowful, to devote himself to the service of his neighbor and the unhappy. There was   yet   another quality which made him beloved; this was the simplicity of his manner, wherein never appeared the shadow of duplicity or dissimulation.   Let us imitate as far as we   can, the example of our Father, and let us return thanks to our Redeemer, who has given such a guide that we may walk in the same path."   (Words of Blessed Jordan of Saxony, first successor of our Holy Father Dominic)

SECTION II.

163. OF THE BOARDING SCHOOL AND OF THE GENERAL MISTRESS.

164. In all the Houses to which a Boarding School is attached, there shall be a general Mistress, charged with the direction and moral education of the pupils. The general Mistress shall be appointed by the Council of the Prioress. She should possess solid virtue, upright judgment, a firm and conciliating spirit. She shall have the management of all that concerns the education of the children, the good order of the school, and those offices which the different teachers discharge. In order to act with prudence and according to the grace of God, she shall have a perfect understanding with her Superior, shall endeavor to have only one thought and one will with her, shall keep her minutely informed of the state of the Academy, and shall decide nothing of importance without her permission. She shall make every effort to preserve unity, charity and harmony between the teachers and pupils, by

sustaining the authority of the former and the helplessness of the latter.

165. On their part, the Mistresses shall give up all self-love and all attachment to their own ideas, to preserve unity, so precious and indispensable in the government of a school, knowing that the amount of good which they may do for the pupils, is in proportion to their union with the general Mistress. It is to her that each Mistress, both Professed and Novice, should give an account of her observations upon the piety, character and labors of the pupils. They ought not to attempt any change under pretext of improvement, without being authorized thereto by the general Mistress; and if the circumstance is important, the latter shall refer it to the Prioress. The Prioress may, in case of need, dispense some teachers whom she knows to be too much occupied, from assisting at Office in Choir, or even, in extraordinary cases, from the private recitation of certain parts of the Office.

Chapter XII.

166. OF LETTERS.

167. No Sister may send or receive letters, or anything written on a piece of paper and unsealed, or anything written on tablets or on wax, without leave, or without showing it to the Conventual Prioress, the Mother General, or to higher Superiors.

168. When the Mother General is present in a Convent, all letters sent or received are to be brought to her, according as she may appoint, and she can open and inspect them, if she think proper, even those addressed to the Prioress.

169. If any Sister, even an immediate Superior, should impede, delay, or open without leave, letters from Superiors to subjects or from subjects to Superiors, or letters from higher Superiors to those of lower rank, or vice versa, she would commit a most grievous offense, both morally and religiously considered, and would be subject to the penalties of the

more grievous fault and of denunciation to the chief Superior. Letters addressed to Superiors should not be read by any one, even if sent or found open.

170. Superiors must not renounce the right which they possess of reading the letters, which their subjects receive or send, and must make no exception for any one whatsoever.

171. The letters which the Religious write to their Sisters in other Convents of the Congregation are not exempt from this rule. They ought to be carefully read at least by the Superioress of the Convent from which they are sent, and if any letters or parcels be entrusted to a Sister going to a Convent, she must not on her arrival deliver them to the Sisters to whom they are addressed, but must give them into the hands of the Prioress.

172. No letters written in the name of the Community shall be sealed with the seal of the Convent, until they have been seen and heard by all the Community. The seal of the Convent must be kept in the chest of the Deposit, by the Depositaries.

173. If it be necessary that any common letter should be signed, or that the consent of

the Sisters should be given to anything, it cannot be done unless those who sign a document
or give consent to any matter of business, be
assembled in one place.   They are also bound
to see and know what is written, and what the
letters or documents contain, under pain of the
more grievous fault.

174. It is strictly forbidden under severe
penalty, to write anonymous letters to Superiors, especially if they be such as affect the
character of any one.

175. The Mistress of Novices has the right
to read the letters of the Novices.   The letters
of the Postulants are subject to the same law
as those of the Novices.

176. No unnecessary letters shall be written
or received during Lent and Advent.

Chapter XIII.

SECTION I.

178. OF SILENCE.

179. The Sisters shall keep silence in the Oratory, Dormitory, Refectory, Cells and Cemetery. But elsewhere they may speak with special permission, in the manner and at the time that shall be allowed them. If any one shall speak from necessity, in a low voice and briefly, she shall not be considered to have broken silence.

180. The Prioress must be careful not to give leave to speak too easily, and without reasonable cause. She may, however, give a general leave to speak, to the cellarer, the cooks and other officers, as shall seem to her expedient. No one should have permission to speak to externs and seculars, or to enter the

parlor, during time of Office and Mass, or after the Community has retired to rest, unless for some necessary cause.

181. No Sister shall speak at the door or in the porch of the church without urgent necessity.

182. Silence must be especially observed at table so that any one who breaks silence at table in the Refectory, shall be penanced as for a grievous fault, nor can any Superior give leave to speak in the Refectory.

183. From the signal for the deep silence which is given with the bell at bedtime, until after Prime, all shall keep silence. When this signal has been given, the Sisters shall retire to their cells, nor must any one presume to enter the cell of another, or go to any Superioress without real necessity; but let deep silence be observed in the cells as in the Dormitory. The sick who are not confined to bed are bound to the observance of the deep silence.

184. When the Sisters go out to visit the sick, they should keep silence in the street, unless it be necessary to give a brief reply, when addressed by any person.

185. The Sisters who are employed in the Schools and other Institutions attached to the Convent, are not dispensed from the law of silence, and must avoid all unnecessary conversation with one another during the hours of silence. They should receive visitors, however, with all courtesy, especially the priests in charge of the Mission, but must not needlessly protract conversation; but if any person apply to them on business, they should, when it is possible, appoint another time and place, so as not to suffer the duties of their office to be hindered.

186. Each Sister, on entering upon her office, must ask the Prioress for necessary leave to speak, which are understood to last a month, and which, even if required permanently, must be renewed at the month's end.

187. The Sisters shall accuse themselves in Chapter of breaking silence, as of their other external faults against the rule and Constitutions, and the Prioress must impose penance according to her discretion. But if any one shall have broken deep silence seven times between two Chapters, she shall sit on the ground during one dinner. Those who sit on the

ground for breaking silence are not bound to fast on bread and water, but only to sit on the ground and eat what the others eat. And this penance must be at dinner, and not at supper. Nor are they to sit on the bare ground, but on a low stool, and they shall have a table or wooden bench on which to eat.

188. That the Sisters may better understand what great account our Fathers made of the Holy Law of silence, that salutary ordinance so conducive to the reformation, peace and good estate of Convents, let them know, that from the year 1242 to 1305, more than twenty General Chapters labored at the arrangement and Confirmation of this part of the Constitutions. And from those ancient times the observance of silence has been over and over again most earnestly inculcated in our laws; and the consciences of Superiors charged in the day of Jesus Christ, if they should fail to impose due penances on those who rashly break it.

189. In accordance with the custom introduced into the most regular Orders, the Sisters shall be allowed an hour's recreation after dinner, and another after supper. If in conse ·

quence of their active occupations some Sisters are often deprived of their midday recreation, the Prioress must endeavor so to regulate the evening employments that all may be able to meet for an hour's recreation after supper.

SECTION II.

190. OF THE PARLOR AND RELATIONS WITH EXTERNS.

191. No Sister may go to the parlor to speak to Seculars without a companion, unless by permission of the Prioress. This permission may be given in the case of near relations, persons well known to the Community, or such as require religious instruction, and other similar cases; but the Prioress must very rarely allow Sisters to go unaccompanied to speak with men, whether priests or laymen.

192. In all that regards communication with externs, the Prioress herself must set an example to the Sisters, and the Mother General must carefully watch over the observance of this part of the Rule.

As the communication of Nuns with externs, and especially with men, may easily become the

cause of dangerous abuses, the Holy See and
General Chapters have vied with one another
in framing the severest ordinances to prevent
such abuses, and to regulate the intercourse of
the Sisters, even with the Religious of their
own Order. Thus it was decreed at Rome,
A. D. 1538: " We prohibit and will have utterly taken away all friendship and familiarities
of our Brethren with Nuns, as well of our own
as of any other Order; and, on the other hand,
of the Sisters with the Brethren of our own or
any other Order, or with any secular person
whatsoever. And if any religious woman shall
in future contract such friendships, or carry
them on by letters or gifts, she shall be disqualified from holding any office, and those
who refuse to correct themselves shall be deprived of all voice and of the veil." These
ordinances were doubtless framed for enclosed
Nuns of the Second Order. Nevertheless,
similar prohibitions, under severe penalties,
were enacted in 1513 by Cardinal Gaetano,
when General of the Order, and expressly extended to women of the Third Order, bound
by simple vows and living in Community. Let
the Sisters, then, conform to these directions in

order to preserve their Convents from abuses, which are more dangerous and more easily introduced than can be understood by those who have not had experience of them.

These wise restrictions give us a correct idea of the religious spirit which should guide the intercourse of Sisters with the world. The further they keep from exposing themselves to the public view, and from every worldly distraction and useless acquaintances, the truer they will be to their sublime vocation.

193. It will be always in accordance with their Rule and Constitutions to take a moderate walk in an unfrequented place for healthy exercise, especially in company with their pupils. The going to private houses, in cities particularly, should be entirely avoided, unless in certain cases deemed by the Prioress necessary on account of some uncommon occurrence.

194. The Sisters shall rarely, and only under strict necessity, go into stores to trade.

195. In case of the sickness or death of parents, Sisters cannot be allowed to visit their homes, except with permission from the Mother General or the Bishop of the place.

196. The receiving of unnecessary visits

should be avoided as much as possible, because more or less they are great distractions in the way of perfection. But, as all Convents of this Order in the United States, on account of the Schools they keep, are bound to have frequent intercourse with the world, it will be the duty of the Council to appoint such Sisters to speak to the strangers as are capable of receiving and conversing with them in an edifying way. Religious, desirous to converse with the world, soon lose the spirit of their vocation. Hence it should always be rather a great mortification than a pleasure to be at times obliged to entertain seculars, whom they should edify by their modest behavior and prudent discourse. Seculars coming from the company of a Sister should carry with them the conviction that Religious are the happiest and the holiest persons in the world, and that they are truly deserving of full confidence in the education of young girls.

Chapter XIV.

SECTION I.

198. OF POSTULANTS.

199. When any Postulant applies for reception, it is the duty of the Mother General to make careful inquiry regarding her character, family, health, means of support, and her motives for desiring the religious life; and if possible, there should be a personal interview before she is accepted. The Council of the Congregation should be consulted, and their consent obtained.

200. No one can be received as a Postulant who is married, even if she have been separated from her husband by the authority of the Church; nor any one who is in debt or who belongs or has belonged to another Religious Order, either as Sister or Novice, or who has

any infirmity, whether manifest or secret, which would unfit her for religious life.

Widows, and ladies over forty years of age shall not be admitted as Candidates unless in extraordinary cases of eminent piety and humility, having, besides, at least one thousand dollars in money, or property to that amount free of all legal difficulties, to give to the Community at the time of their Profession. This requisite is a just compensation to the Convent ·for the support of such members, who are of little service and an expense to the House. In general, persons advanced in life, on account of their past mode of living are seldom pleased with the ways of a Community, hence it will be more prudent to refuse such. No one can be received who is necessary for the support of her parents, as the Angelic Doctor teaches; nor must any one be admitted with faults which appear to be innate or almost insuperable, such as violent anger and the like, of which there can be scarcely any hope of cure; nor those who show any disposition to insanity; nor any not of good character.

201. None who are ignorant and incapable of learning can be received as Sisters. No one

can be received on condition of not being removed from one particular Convent, or for any special occupation, and if any should be received on such condition, the condition shall be null and void. More than usual care must be taken, for the reception of those who are very young, of recent converts from heresy, of those whose birth is illegitimate, and of the children of ill-conducted parents; but if such be once received and professed, they are eligible to all the offices of the Congregation without further dispensation.

202. Those who have made profession, or who have even worn the habit in another Order, or in another Congregation of our own Order cannot be received without a dispensation from the Mother General with her Council. Nor can any Novice who has laid aside the habit in our own Congregation, whether of her own accord or not, be re-admitted to our Novitiate without a similar dispensation. Any such person must not be allowed to live always in any of our Convents, that is, as forming part of the Community.

SECTION II.

204. Whatever a Postulant brings to the Convent, such as books, clothing, etc., beyond what is required for her actual use, must be put into a place apart under lock and key, and kept until her Profession, in order that it may be returned to her without difficulty if she should not persevere. The Holy Council of Trent enjoins as follows: " Before the Profession of a Novice, nothing shall be given to the Monastery out of her property, either by parents, relatives or guardians, under any pretext whatever, except for food and clothing for the time that she is under probation, lest the said Novice be unable to leave on this account; that the Monastery is in possession of the whole, or of the greater part of her substance, and she may not easily be able to recover it if she should leave. Yea, rather, the Holy Synod enjoins, under the pain of anathema, that this be nowise done; and that to those who leave before their Profession, everything that was theirs be restored; and the Bishop shall, if

need be, enforce by ecclesiastical censures that this be performed in a proper manner." (Sess. 25, ch. xviii.)

205. It is also forbidden to Postulants and Novices to dispose of the goods or property which belong to them during the whole time of their probation, until the two months which precede their Profession; this prohibition does not, however; extend to little gifts which do not notably diminish the property of the Novice.

206. During the two months which precede Profession the Novice must make arrangements with regard to all her property present and to come. And she must place in the hands of the Mother General a signed document, stating all the engagements which she or her parents have made with regard to the Congregation, and the Mother General shall keep this paper in the Archives of the Congregation. But these engagements shall be regarded as taking effect only in the event of Profession being actually made, and must be sanctioned by the Ordinary of the place, the Mother General and her Council. Any renunciation contrary to this, even though made with an oath, is declared to be null and void.

207. If á Novice should leave the Institute, or die before Profession, the Convent cannot keep such portion of her property as has been made over to it, even in the prescribed form ; since, as the ·Profession has not taken place, the gift or renunciation is null and void. But a legacy or devise or any disposition by last will or testament óf or made by the Novice of her property, would not come under the prohibition of the Council.

208. The act which constitutes a Postulant is the signing of the following agreement :

We, the undersigned, who may sign this instrument at separate times, do each for herself, declare and agree as follows :

I, the undersigned, have asked to be received and was received by this Community of Sisters of St. Dominic, St. Clara's Convent, as a Postulant, in the hope of becoming, in due time, a life member of the same. Now, I do hereby promise, and, in a special manner agree, with, and before, all the Sisters representing this Community and Convent, that if, at any time after the date written under my name, this Sisterhood or Convent or my Superior in the Community, shall request me to leave the House, the Com-

munity, or the Institute itself, I shall quietly, and without complaint, obey, and leave it, as requested, without asking or claiming at any time, any compensation for whatever work I may have done, or for whatever money or goods or property of any kind, I may have given to the Community, Convent, or any body corporate, whose affairs may be conducted by the Community or by any member or members thereof or that I may have given for the use of the Community, Convent or for the purposes of the Institute; and I do hereby acknowledge that my board and lodging, clothing, support, and maintenance during my stay in this Institute, are all and the full compensation and legal payment I ask, claim or expect, and these I have agreed and do hereby freely agree to take and accept as and for full payment and compensation for all said work or donations, grants or gifts.

209. This formula of agreement shall be written in the Book of Records, and every Postulant shall sign it with her name, or signature, and with the date. Each signature shall be certified by three Sisters, as witnesses. The Book of Records shall be kept carefully for a reference before any civil tribunal, if necessary.

All this should be done to avoid serious difficulties, which might arise from the wickedness of the world in case of expulsion.

SECTION III.

210 OF THE LAWFUL MANNER OF RECEIVING TO THE HABIT.

211. The length of the postulancy is left to the discretion of the Mother General and her Council, but should not be less than six months.

212. The year of probation cannot begin before the age of fifteen years complete

213. Two months before the Clothing the Postulant should be examined in private by two Examiners, chosen from the Mothers of Council. She should be examined on the principal truths of faith, and on the duties of the holy state which she desires to embrace. She shall be asked in what spirit and with what intention she has made choice of this manner of life; what end she has proposed to herself; whether she has been led to embrace it out of desire for a more perfect life, in order to serve

God more easily ; or whether, on the other hand, she has chosen it lightly, or has been influenced by any human affection, or other improper motive. The Examiner should also, with gentleness and kindness, inquire into those points which would prove obstacles to her reception, and on which full information has not yet been obtained.

214. After the Examiners have made their report of this examination to the Mother General and her Council, and the Mistress of Novices has faithfully said all she may have remarked in the Postulant regarding her inclinations and aptitude for religious life, the Council shall vote by secret suffrage on the reception of the Postulant, before proposing her to the Community, and if she has not the majority of votes, she cannot be admitted. If, on the contrary, she obtains the majority of votes, the consent of the Ordinary must be obtained.

215. All the professed Sisters living in the Novitiate House have the right of voting for the reception of Postulants to the Habit, and of Novices to Profession; but a Religious who has been absent from the Novitiate House

more than six months loses the right of voting until after two months of renewed residence.

216. It is, moreover, necessary to give a month's notice before the Clothing to the Bishop of the Diocese, that he may himself, or by a delegate, examine the Postulant, to see if she is acting under constraint or by persuasion, and if she thoroughly understands what she is doing. The same must be done in regard to Novices before their Profession. But, if the Bishop does not examine, after fifteen days from the time the notice was given, steps may be taken for the Profession of the Novice at the time appointed.

217. Postulants must make a spiritual Retreat of eight days before their Clothing.

218. The Mother General alone has the right to present Postulants for the Holy Habit to the Superior, and to receive Novices to Profession. No other Sister can do this, except by delegation from her, but when there is no Mother General, the Vicaress General has this right.

219. The Scapular is not to be blessed until Profession.

220. It is customary for the Novices to wear a white veil until Profession.

221. A Plenary Indulgence may be gained on condition of Confession and Communion, by Postulants on receiving the habit, and by Novices on making Profession.

222. As soon as the Postulant has taken the Habit, the Mistress of Novices must register her Clothing in the Book of Clothings and Professions, with her age and the day and hour at which the Clothing took place.

223. From the time of her Clothing, a Religious must always put the word Sister before her own name, and must do the same in speaking of others.

Chapter XV.

OF THE NOVICES AND OF THEIR INSTRUCTION.

SECTION I.

224. OF THE NOVITIATE.

225. Nothing is so necessary in order to promote unity of spirit and uniformity of observance so essential to a Religious Institute, as that all should be formed upon the same model, and educated in one common Novitiate. There is, therefore, but one house of Novitiate in our Congregation, to which all the Houses shall send the Postulants received by them, at least until the Congregation shall be divided into Provinces.

226. The Postulant before receiving the Habit must make a spiritual Retreat of eight days during which she will have no communication with any one except the Confessor, the Superioress and the Mistress of Novices.

during this time of Retreat, she will examine her vocation ; she will also make a general Confession unless the Confessor decide otherwise.

227. Before she is clothed, she must give in writing signed with her name, that she comes by her own free choice, and not by compulsion or persuasion, and that she is willing to conform to the Rules and Customs.

228. The time of Novitiate in our Congregation is one full year, from the day of reception to the Habit. The Novitiate may be prolonged for just cause, but it can never be shortened except in case of Profession *in articulo mortis*, in which case, should the Novice recover, she should complete the time of her Novitiate, before Professing in the ordinary manner.

229. No one, even if she hold some office in the community, can enter the Novitiate without permission of the Mistress of Novices or of higher Superiors, except the Mother-General, or Conventual Prioress, when they may deem it to be expedient. The Mistress of Novices cannot give leave to any one to enter the Novitiate, except for some necessary or useful purpose.

230. The Novices cannot speak to the Pro-

fessed Sisters, except when necessity requires. During the Novitiate and time of Probation the Novices shall not associate with the Professed Sisters, except in Choir, in the Church, in Processions, and in the Refectory. To these and other public places they shall go together. The other members of the House shall hold communication with them through the Mistress.

231. It may be prudent on certain occasions that a Novice should be allowed to speak with her relations and friends; but this should be done in the presence of the Religious companion approved by the Superior. Parents and guardians may be allowed to see a Novice without a companion.

232. In everything the Novices must learn to be utterly dependent on their Superiors, like little children, for, "of such is the Kingdom of Heaven," stripping themselves of all self-will and in its stead, putting on the Lord Jesus Christ.

233. The Novices should not be sent to other Houses, out of the Novitiate, before Profession, unless when ordered by a physician for a short time, for the sake of health.

SECTION II.

234. OF THE MISTRESS OF NOVICES.

235. Forasmuch as from the holy and approved education of Novices, great advantages result to religion, and regular discipline is wonderfully propagated, the Mistress of Novices should be chosen with most careful solicitude. And no one ought to excuse herself from the exercise of an office which is so important and so necessary for religion.

236. The Mistress of Novices should be prudent and mature, well versed in the chant and ceremonies of the Order, and capable of instructing the Novices in those things which they will have to practice when Professed. She must be free from all offices and employments which could be a hindrance to the proper care of the Novices; she must be at least thirty years of age, and seven years professed; she must be well instructed, of exemplary life, given to prayer and works of mortification, prudent and charitable, uniting affability with gravity, have a zeal for God tempered with meekness; as far

as possible removed from all passion, especially from anger and impatience; one, in short, who is fitted to give them an example of every virtue, and who will seek rather to be loved than feared by them.

237. The Mistress ought to provide her Novices with all that is necessary for them, as far as lies in her power.

238. The Novice Mistress ranks next to the Sub-Prioress, but for greater convenience she shall be near the Novices in Choir, Refectory and Processions.

239. She is, by right, a member of both the General and Conventual Councils, and is exempt from the office of Hebdomadaria.

240. The Mistress of Novices has full and absolute authority in all that concerns the instruction of the Novices and the administration of the Novitiate, and no one except her Superiors can interfere in these matters. Nevertheless, the Mistress shall consider it a duty to consult her Superiors concerning the government of the Novitiate, and give them an account of all that concerns it. The chief superintendence of the Novitiate belongs to the Mother General.

241. As the duration of the office of Mistress of Novices is not fixed by any law, she shall continue in office until removed by Superiors.

242. If the number of Novices require it, a Sub-Mistress may be appointed, who should, as far as possible, have the same qualifications as the Mistress.

SECTION III.

243. OF THE INSTRUCTION OF THE NOVICES.

244. The Mistress of Novices must take care all the Novices are exercised in regular discipline, that they know how to value the excellence of the divine vocation with which they have been favored, and that they understand the true observance of the essentials of Religion: Poverty, Chastity and Obedience. They must also be instructed in the Rules and Constitutions of the Order, which they must learn to prize and observe faithfully as the great means of their salvation and perfection. Each Novice should have a book of the Constitutions, and should study it with care, the better to understand the obligations of our laws.

245. The Novices should also be taught the manner of making mental and vocal prayer. They should also, with all diligence acquire habits of recollection, of keeping themselves in the presence of God, of great modesty and custody of the senses and of union with God by frequent aspiratory prayer and purity of intention. They must be instructed as to the necessity of general and particular examination of conscience, and how to make it with profit, also how to prepare for Confession. In order to assist their spiritual advancement, they should be made to study the Lives of the Saints of our Order, and the Spiritual works of St. Bernard, St. Vincent Ferrer, St. Catharine of Sienna, B. Humbert, the Venerable Louis of Granada, etc.

246. They will, moreover, apply themselves to the practice of the essential virtues of self-denial and mortification of the senses, humility and perfect obedience, and frequent opportunities of exercising these virtues should be afforded them. The Mistress shall often exercise her Novices in low and menial employments, in order to form them to humility of heart and body, according to these words of our Lord:

" Learn of Me, for I am meek and humble of heart." She shall teach them to live without possessing anything as their own; to take great care of the books, clothes, and other things belonging to the Convent; to renounce their own wills, to obey their Mistress and all their Superiors in all things, and never to presume to dispute with any one, but to render a prompt and willing obedience. If one Superioress have refused them anything, they must be taught never to ask the same thing of another, without mentioning that it has been refused them; and if a Superioress of higher authority have refused them, they must not ask it afterward from one in inferior authority.

247. They must learn to watch over the affections, detaching themselves from creatures, and avoiding with strictest care, all particular friendships; whilst, on the other hand, they must be sweet and amiable to all, not insisting upon their own opinion, but endeavoring in indifferent matters, to conform to the views and tastes of others, lest the bond of charity be broken. Correction and reproof they must learn to receive with all humility, being slow to justify themselves when wrongly accused

except where charity or edification requires it.

248. The Mistress of Novices shall be careful to instruct them how to behave everywhere and under all circumstances. She shall teach them to keep silence in the times and places appointed; not to speak without permission; not to talk too much, but to restrain their tongues, and wherever they may be, not to talk foolishly, but of things profitable. The Mistress shall further recommend them never to pass judgment on any one, but whatever action they may see done, to consider it good, or, at least, done with a good intention, though it may appear bad, because the judgment of man is often deceived.

249. The Novices shall not be present at the Chapter of Faults of the Community, but shall accuse themselves at the beginning of it, and the Mistress shall proclaim them if there is cause; or else she shall hear their faults in the Chapter of the Novitiate, giving them penances when they accuse themselves of their outward negligences, and correcting them with kindness and charity.

250. The Novices should, if possible, every day, be present at the Conventual Mass, and

assist at the Office in Choir.   They must carefully study the recitation of the Office, and
their Mistress should teach them, in a regular
and methodical manner, the ceremonies, that is
to say, the inclinations and prostrations, and all
that belongs to religion, that they may advance
at once in knowledge and good discipline.

251. Since one principal object of the Congregation is to teach the doctrines of our Holy
Religion to the poor and ignorant, great care
must be taken during the term of Novitiate,
that all the Sisters be thoroughly instructed in
it themselves.   The Novices must be particularly examined on this point before Profession ;
and their Profession must be deferred, if they
are found not sufficiently instructed.

252. It has always been the custom in our
Congregation, approved by our first Superiors,
to allow the Novices and the Postulants to
assist both in the Schools and in the domestic
offices of the Convent, during the time of their
probation, in order that they may the better
know what they are undertaking by their Profession.   But these occupations must never be
allowed to interfere with the instruction and
exercises of the Novitiate.

253. But it must be remembered that our Congregation is primarily devoted to education as the means of securing the sanctification of our own souls, and the good of our neighbor, and everything should tend to promote that end. Therefore, the Novices and Postulants whom the Community or Council intend to employ in the Schools, whether Parochial or Boarding Schools, in any capacity, should receive intelligent and systematic training, sufficient to fit them for this important duty, and this should be of obligation. Moreover, they should understand that the duty of mental improvement lasts while they continue to be employed as teachers.

254. All the Novices must be occupied either in learning or doing some work which will be useful to the Community.

255. They shall be allowed some modest recreation twice a day, which may be prolonged a little once every week or fortnight. The Mistress or her companion must be present at the recreation, and must take care that two do not remain together apart from the rest; and at these times they should take occasion to observe the habits and natural disposition of each.

256. Whenever Novices wish to return to the world or to go to another Monastery, we command all the Religious freely to let them go and to return to them all they have brought. Nor must any reproach them on this account, but follow the example of Him, who, when some of His disciples went back, said to those that remained: "Will you also go away?"

SECTION IV.

257. OF THE TERM OF PROBATION.

The term of Probation cannot begin until the Postulant has completed her fifteenth year.

258. The time of Probation must be reckoned from the moment of taking the habit, but if, from any circumstance, a Postulant should receive the habit in a Convent other than the Novitiate-house, the term of Probation must be reckoned, not from the day and hour of her taking the habit, but from her entrance into the Novitiate-house.

259. The year of Probation must be not only complete, but continuous; consequently, if any person should persevere in the Institute during six months, and should afterward leave, and

then return to it again after some time, she could not be Professed at the end of another six months; but she would be obliged to begin again and continue for one consecutive year, because otherwise she could not be said to have really made trial of the difficulties of the religious life, which mainly consist in their continuance.

260. A Novice who shall be judged by the Physicians to be at the point of death, may, for the comfort of her soul, make her Profession, even though she have not entirely accomplished her term of Probation. The Sovereign Pontiff St. Pius V., of happy memory, granted this favor to Novices of the Order of St. Dominic, that they might gain the Indulgence attached to Religious Profession.

261. The same holy Pontiff has declared that the Profession of such persons as are considered not yet fit to be Professed may be delayed for six months after the expiration of their time of probation, if there be any hope that during that six months they will become capable of it; but when those six months are expired, if they are not then found fit to be Professed they must be sent away from the Convent. The

Profession of a Novice may, nevertheless, be deferred even beyond two years, if the Monastery has not yet received the dowry agreed upon.

262. During the period of Probation the Institute is free to send the Novice away, and she is also free to leave the Institute. No Novice can be deprived of the habit except by the Mother General with her Council, unless in an urgent case ; and then the Local Superior must immediately render an account of her act to the Mother General.

263. Within two months of the completion of her term of Probation, the Novice must be examined, as we have already said of Postulants before their Clothing ; but the Novice must be examined also on the Rule, the Constitutions and the recitation of the Office ; and no one shall be received to Profession who has not a sufficient knowledge of all these things. Before a Novice can be received to Profession the same formalities are required as before receiving her to the habit, and the same questions and protestations must be made, and Superiors who are negligent on this point incur the penalty of the more grievous fault.

264. If the Superior or the Mother General were to admit a Sister to Profession, contrary to the votes of the majority of the Chapter, the Profession would be null.

265. Let all those who have to give their votes for the admission of Novices to Profession, take heed to the serious admonition of the Chapter of Ghent, A. D. 1871, regarding this important duty: " Considering the special need there is in our days, of prudent severity in the admission of subjects to religion, we exhort all those who have a right to vote for the Profession of Novices, to admit to Profession none but those who are worthy and approved. They should have one thing only before their eyes in giving their votes, namely: whether the Novice in question has shown such clear and manifest signs of a true and Divine vocation, and of fidelity in walking worthy of it, as that she may be safely admitted to Profession; if not, she ought either to be sent back to the world, or at least her Profession should be deferred, as shall seem best in the Lord."

266. The Novices must make a spiritual retreat of eight days before Profession.

267. After Profession, the Novice must her-

self sign the act of her engagement in the Book of Clothings and Professions. If a Sister cannot write, she must make a cross with her own hand at the foot of the act, which must be written for her. The age of the Novice Professed, together with the year, month, day and hour of her Profession, must also be set down, as well as the name of the Superioress who received her Profession.

The Novice must further add that she has made Profession of her own free will. This act must be signed by the Mother General, the Mistress of Novices, and another Sister. The Ecclesiastical Superior or his delegate, and those who have assisted at the ceremony may also be requested to sign. The Book must be preserved in the Archives of the Congregation.

CHAPTER XVI.

OF PROFESSION.

SECTION I.

268. OF THE FORM OF PROFESSION AND OF THE NATURE OF THE VOWS.

269. The following is the manner of making Profession:

" To the honor of Almighty God, Father, Son and Holy Ghost, and of the Blessed Virgin Mary, and of the Blessed Dominic, I, Sister N, called in the world N. N., make my Profession, and promise obedience to Almighty God, to the Blessed Virgin Mary, to the Blessed Dominic, and to you, Sister N., Mother-General, of the American Congregation of the Most Holy Rosary, of the Third Order of St. Dominic, according to the Rule of Saint Augustine and the Institutions of the American Congregation of the Most Holy Rosary, that I will be obedient to you and my other Prioresses, even unto death."

270. Although in the above form of Profession the vow of obedience only is expressed, yet under it are included the other two vows of chastity and voluntary poverty, which we bind ourselves to observe.

271. Every Religious of our Institute is bound, in virtue of her vocation to the religious state, to strive, as far as lies in her power, to live according to the Rule and Constitutions which we profess, as we have each expressly promised to God in the form of Profession. Profession makes a person a Religious, and places her in a state of Perfection. Now, a person is said to be in a state of perfection, not inasmuch as she has actually attained to the perfection of charity, but inasmuch as she obliges herself forever, and with solemnity, to those things, that belong to perfection. And Religious are in a state of perfection, because they are obliged forever, to those things which belong to perfection. For Religious take upon them the state of perfection, not as professing to be perfect, but as professing to be tending toward perfection.

272. Profession must be made in public, in the Chapter Room or in the Church.

273. At Profession the Scapular is blessed; and when Sisters, already Professed, get new Scapulars, they must have them blessed by some Priest having the necessary faculties. The Scapular has been enriched by the Sovereign Pontiff John XXII., with an indulgence of five years and five quarantines, which may be gained by kissing it devoutly. The Scapular does not lose the blessing and indulgence when given successively to the use of several Sisters.

SECTION II.

274. ON POVERTY AND COMMUNITY OF GOODS.

275. All ought to be common in our Institute, as well food and clothing as furniture and linen. Each Sister shall receive from the Sister charged by the Superior all that is needful. The Professed Sisters can keep the radical dominion of their goods, inasmuch as the Profession of the Simple Vows does not destroy such dominion. It is, however, absolutely prohibited to keep the administration, use and

profit of them. Before Profession, the Sisters must surrender to whomever they shall think best, it may be to the Institute, the administration, the profit, the use of their goods. In the act of surrender the Sisters may add the stipulation that this surrender is revocable at their option, but they cannot use this privilege, that is, of revoking this surrender, without first having obtained permission for it from the Sacred Congregation of the Propaganda. The same rule must be followed in regard to the property which the Sisters may acquire after their Profession, by title of inheritance or of donation. As regards the radical dominion, therefore, the Sisters can dispose either by will or with donation, but always with the permission of the Superioress General. This giving up of radical dominion with donation, shall annul the act of surrender made as to the administration, profit, use; unless the Sisters declare that this surrender is to exist notwithstanding the donation of radical dominion. It is permitted to the Professed Sisters to execute, with the permission of the Mother General, the acts of property required by law. The Sisters, however cannot dispose of the endowment given to the Institute. In order that the vow of Poverty may be more religiously observed, the Superioress General should provide the Sisters in all their needs, both of food and clothing, whether the Sisters be healthy or infirm. The Superioress General ought, moreover, to be vigilant that the Sisters live in conformity with the Vow of Poverty which they have professed. If any Sister should transgress the Vow of Poverty in giving retaining or receiving any object of importance, without the permission of the proper Superior, she ought to be severely punished.

276. Superiors cannot give permission to the Sisters to give the things which have been granted for their use, to persons out of the Order, to keep for them.

277. No Sister can beg of any one whatsoever, without leave, general or special, from her Superior.

278. If any Sister shall receive precious objects, or money, as alms, or for any other purpose, she is bound within the space of twenty-four hours to present them to the Superioress, or to those officers who are authorized to receive them. Superiors of Houses or Convents

are themselves not exempt from this law. If collections be received for pious or charitable purposes, the money must not be kept by the Prioress, but must be consigned to the Bursar within the space of twenty-four hours from the time of its reception, that it may be laid up in the common Deposit.

279. All Sisters, except Conventual Prioresses, who are guests in one of our Convents, are bound to consign their money to the common Deposit, if their stay be prolonged beyond six days.

280. Those Sisters who have the administration of money are bound to render an account of it to their Superiors at least once a year, or oftener if required of them. The Mother General must give an account of her administration to the Diffinitresses of the General Chapter; the Conventual Prioresses to the Mother General, and the other Sisters to the Conventual Prioresses.

281. Once every year, or oftener, if it shall be required of them, the Sisters are bound to lay everything which has been given them for their use, at the feet of their Superioress, or, at least, to put everything faithfully down in

writing without concealing anything, and to present the writing to their Superiors, thus stripping themselves of all property in any-thing whatsoever. The time prescribed for doing this is the month of December. These inventories must not be given to the Superioress sealed, but open.

282. No Sister shall appropriate to herself anything whatsoever, not so much as a cup or vase, or anything of that kind. Also no Sister may have a chest, or anything whatever, with a lock and key, excepting those who cannot do without it on account of their offices.

283. The Prioress, in company with any Sister whom she may choose, shall examine the cells of the Sisters, in their absence, when-ever she shall think proper, and if she shall find there anything which a Religious is keep-ing without leave, she shall take it away, and impose a penance on that Sister proportioned to her fault.

284. No Sister shall have spoons, or any other things made of silver or gold or precious stones, under the penalty of being deprived of these objects, which shall be applied to the benefit of the Community.

Those Sisters who are obliged, on account of their offices, to have watches, are permitted to have them made of silver. Silver thimbles are allowed, especially when the nature of the work requires it. One or two silver spoons may be kept in the Infirmary, for the administration of certain remedies that require it, but silver must not be used for the ordinary service of the sick. Silver spoons, etc., may be provided for the use of guests.

285. Superiors, who should show themselves an example of good works to their subjects, shall be careful to embrace this voluntary poverty themselves; putting far from them all vanities and superfluities, which they cannot approve in others, as regards clothing, food, the furniture of their rooms, their journeys, etc., that so they may lead those committed to their care by the shortest road to religious perfection.

286. Those Sisters who have the administration of the goods of the Convent, such as Syndics, Bursars, Cellarers, Librarians, Habit-Mistresses and Sacristans, ought faithfully to manage all those things which are intrusted to them for the common good. Nor ought the

Sisters to seek any remuneration for exercising these or any other offices in the Convent, since all their works, and even their wills, are subject to their Superiors.

287. Those Sisters who have contracted debts must be severely punished.

288. Perfect Community life being so useful a means of promoting piety, that where it is in vigor, religion is wont to flourish, and to bring forth almost as many saints as it has professed members, Superiors are bound to maintain it, with the utmost diligence, and not to permit the slightest opening through which it may escape from their Communities, and those who are negligent, or too indulgent, in this most essential part of their duty, should be removed from office. Subjects, also, ought not to resist their Superiors in this matter ; for if they make resistance, because 'they wish to dispose of what they have according to their own pleasure, they are evidently in a dangerous state.

SECTION III.

290. The Religious should ever bear in mind, that being consecrated to God by the vow of Chastity, their whole demeanor, as our Father St. Augustine says in the Rule, should be such as becomes the sanctity of their state. All unnecessary intercourse, therefore, and undue familiarity with those of the other sex, should be carefully avoided, and the regulations concerning their intercourse with externs, whether secular or Religious, should be carefully observed.

291. Although the Religious of this Congregation, not being enclosed, are permitted to go out of their Convent with leave, for works of charity and necessity, yet within the Convent a certain enclosure should be observed: that is to say, the garden, and apartments of the Religious, should be so arranged as to be entirely separate from those assigned to the use of the guests, or any Institute attached to the Convent; and no extern, especially persons

of the other sex, shall be admitted within that enclosure without an express permission, which permission must not be too easily granted. The custom of allowing externs to see portions of the Conventual premises, is not here forbidden, but it must never be done without permission of the Prioress, who must take care that the privacy of the Religious is not intruded upon.

In Convents, the buildings of which are still incomplete, this enclosure of the garden and apartments may not be practicable at once; but where Religious are thus left with less exterior protection, the Prioress should be all the more solicitous to maintain in her community, that religious reserve which should serve as a moral enclosure.

292. Except in rare and exceptional cases, no extern should be admitted to the recreations of the Sisters.

293. In every Convent, some discreet Sister of matured and upright character, shall be appointed as Portress, who shall kindly receive visitors when they come to the Convent, and shall pay them suitable attention, while the younger Sister, who is her companion, goes, with permission of the Superioress, to seek the

Religious called for. The Portress shall not permit seculars to go about the Convent. The front door shall always be closed in such a manner that no one can open it from outside. Let there be a tablet with the names of all the Sisters, in some convenient place near the principal door, and let the Portress note, by some sign, when a Sister goes out and when she returns, that she may be able to give an answer when the Sisters are inquired for.

294. The keys of the Convent must be brought every evening to the cell of the Prioress, or sub-Prioress

295. No Sister shall presume to go out, except for some express cause, and with a companion, from whom she must not separate. A Sister must ask permission each time she goes out, and this permission must be granted for some approved cause only. The Superior should appoint a companion for her, and this must not depend on the choice of the Sister going out, but on the judgment of the Superior; nor should the same Sisters be too often assigned as companions. On their return, the Sisters shall present themselves as soon as possible to the Prioress, or sub-Prioress, to give an

account of themselves; this they must do as often as they leave the Convent or return.

296. No Mother General or Local Superior can give a general, vague and indeterminate permission to go out from the Convent, to any Sister whatsoever, whether assigned to that Convent, or only staying there, even if she be a Mother of Council of the Congregation.

297. It is a grievous fault for any Sister to go out of the Convent without permission, or with any other companion than the one assigned her.

SECTION IV.

298. OF OBEDIENCE.

299. Of the three vows of religion, the principal and most essential is that of obedience: first, because by it a greater good is offered to God than by the others, for by obedience we offer to God our will, and the goods of the soul, which are preferable to the bodily and outward goods, which are offered to God by the other vows; secondly, because the vow of obedience

contains in itself the other vows; thirdly, because the vow of obedience properly extends to those things which approach most nearly to the end contemplated by religion, namely, the perfection of charity and the love of God. Now, the nearer anything approaches its end the better it is, and, therefore, in our profession, we express the one vow of obedience only, under which is included the observance of chastity and voluntary poverty, and of all the Ordinances of the Rule and Constitutions, or enjoined by Superiors.

300. First and directly, the obedience which we owe to our Superiors extends to those things, which are explicitly contained in the Rule or Constitutions, or in the ordinances of General Chapters, declared to apply to our Congregation. Secondly and indirectly, we are also bound to obey our Superiors in those things, which, though not contained explicitly in our laws, are nevertheless found to be necessary, or at least very useful, for their observance, such as the community duties, without which the state of religion could not be kept up, the penalties for transgressions, and the ordinances of Superiors, which tend either to pre-

serve or restore regular discipline. But we are not bound—indeed we cannot obey—in those things which are contrary to the precepts of God, or of the Church, or against the Rule, or which do not allow of the dispensations of the Superiors; but in doubtful cases, all are bound to obey.

301. The character of true obedience is taught us by the Venerable Father Humbert, fifth General of the Order, who, in his letter to the Provinces, exhorts all the members of the Order to strive to obey, " promptly and devoutly, as to God and not to man, willingly and simply, without contradiction or discussion, with courage, cheerfulness and exactitude, obey ing every command without exception and with unremitting perseverance."

302. In the form of our Profession we promise obedience, not only to God, whom we are bound to revere in the person of our Superiors, but also to the Blessed Virgin, because it has been proved many times, and in various ways; that she protects the Order of St. Dominic to which we are united. She it was who interceded with her Son when He was angry with the world, and obtained, that this Order should

be instituted to turn men from their sins and errors, and bring them back to the knowledge and love of God. Thus, the Queen of Heaven, the ever-Blessed Virgin is our especial advocate, and our most tender Mother and Patroness, who ever intercedes for us with God, and has often protected and delivered this Order from various disturbances and calamities, as the lives of the Brethren and Sisters narrate. Again, we promise obedience to the Blessed Dominic, our Father, because he was the first Master, institutor and founder of the Order of Preachers; and it was he whom the Blessed Virgin presented to her Son as a faithful and valiant champion, ready to fight against error, and extirpate vice.

303. We are, moreover, bound to obey the Sovereign Pontiff, not only in those things which are common to all the faithful, but also in such as especially belong to regular discipline, as St. Thomas teaches.

304. In case of just necessity, appeals may be made by the Sisters to higher Superiors, from those of inferior authority; and Superiors, thus appealed to are bound to examine and redress the grievances alleged. It is, however,

strictly forbidden for subjects to have recourse to higher Superiors on frivolous pretexts, and in order to evade the obedience due to those immediately placed over them. Nor must higher Superiors encourage or receive appeals of this nature; or excuse, impede, suspend or annul the obedience imposed on subjects, or retard its execution. They should rather guard and support the authority of all subordinate Superiors as carefully as their own, lest by too easily receiving frivolous appeals, that authority be eluded and fall into contempt. The principle of supporting those in subordinate authority, applies equally to all those Conventual offices in which several Sisters are working under the superintendence of one chief Mistress, who is bound to require that all under her charge, whether children in schools or patients in hospitals, shall yield the same respect and obedience to those who assist her in her office as they render to herself.

Chapter XVII.

305. OF FAULTS.

SECTION I.

306. OF LIGHT FAULTS.

307. It is a light fault if any Sister, at the first sound of the bell, does not leave off her occupation, and prepare herself, with becoming diligence, to go in time to the place to which the signal may summon her. If any one does not carefully fulfill the part assigned to her, in reading or singing; or, if she disturbs the Choir by making a mistake in beginning an Anthem, Responsory, or the like. If any one does not immediately humble herself before all when she makes a mistake in reading or singing, by reverently kissing her Scapular, at the same time bowing her head. If the book which is read out of at table, in Chapter, or in Church, be not in its place through the negligence of anyone. It is also a light fault if anyone does not

come in good time to table, or to Sermon, or to Chapter, or Choir, or the common work-room; or, if the Sister appointed to read at table comes too late to ask the blessing. If any one shall make a noise in the Dormitory, or elsewhere in the Convent, or shall disturb the other Sisters in any way when they are praying, reading or working. If the cloths for covering the chalice, or the paten, or the corporal, or stole, or maniple, or the like, shall fall to the ground through the negligence of any one; or if any Sister shall not put away her clothes in a decent, orderly manner, at the time and in the place appointed. It is also a light fault if a Sister shall lose or break a candle, or any utensil, or shall spoil or lose any of her clothes. If any Sister shall go to sleep at Office, at Sermon, or in the work-room, or shall let her eyes wander, and fix them on vain objects whilst going through the Cloisters or the House. If any one shall waste time in idle words, or shall laugh boisterously or incite others to rude laughter or shall appear reprehensible in gesture, movement, posture, habit or word.

For these and similar faults, there shall be enjoined one or more Psalms, or some other penance, at the discretion of whoever holds the Chapter, regard being had to the number and degree of the faults.

SECTION II.

308. OF MIDDLE FAULTS.

309. It is a middle fault if any Sister shall not come into Choir till after the *Gloria Patri* of the first Psalm, and shall not make satisfaction for it by prostrating in the middle of the Choir.

It is a fault of the same kind, if any Sister being inattentive at the Office, shows the levity of her mind, by wandering eyes and irreligious deportment.

If any Sister shall not look over, beforehand, what she has to read in Choir, or shall presume to say or sing anything different from what is appointed.

If any one shall laugh, or make others laugh, in Choir, or shall behave with levity in presence of the Community.

If any Sister shall absent herself from Chapter, or sermon, from the Refectory, the workroom, or the Choir, for an insufficient cause.

If any Sister shall allow her eyes to wander, or fix them on vain things while going through the streets.

If any one shall read forbidden books, that is to say, not those books the reading of which is forbidden to all the faithful of Christ (for to read such is a more grievous fault), but useless worldly books and novels, the reading of which is unbecoming a Religious, who ought to be wholly given to spiritual things.

If any one shall negligently handle the ornaments of the Church or of the Altar.

If any one shall neglect some general command that has been given to the whole Community.

If any one shall eat or drink out of meals without leave and without a blessing.

If any one shall proclaim another Sister by whom she has been herself proclaimed on the same day, as if by way of petty revenge, or shall make her proclamation with temper.

If any one shall affirm or deny anything with any expression resembling an oath (such as is sometimes used in conversation), or shall use words of ridicule.

If any one shall call a Religious by her name, without the title of Sister, habitually.

If any one shall say or do anything which can give offense to the Sisters.

If any Sister shall not return to the Convent at the appointed hour.

If any one shall be negligent in the Office assigned her, as Chantress, Sacristan, Syndica, etc.

For faults of this kind, let Psalms, disciplines, venias, or other penances be imposed, at the discretion of whoever holds the Chapter, regard being had to the number and degree of the faults.

310. The Sisters are forbidden to play at chess, cards, dice, or any game of chance, especially if it be for money, or to act in any kind of play.

SECTION III.

311. OF GRIEVOUS FAULTS.

312. It is a grievous fault if any Religious shall have a quarrel or unseemly contention with another Sister.

If she shall speak insultingly to any one, or

reproach a Sister with a fault for which she has done penance.

If any one shall proclaim another in Chapter, in a violent manner, or shall use rude, intemperate, or improper language towards a Sister by whom she has been proclaimed, or towards any other.

If any one shall sow discord amongst the Sisters, or shall be guilty of detraction, or uncharitable murmurs in secret.

If any one shall maliciously speak evil of the Sisters, or of the Convent, or shall defend with boldness her own fault, or that of another.

If any one shall tell a willful lie, or shall murmur against the food, clothing, or anything else, or shall break silence habitually.

If any Sister eat meat on abstinence days, or break the appointed fasts, without leave or necessity.

If any Sister shall presume to return without permission from any place to which she has been sent, or if she do not return at the appointed time, unless she be delayed by some reasonable cause.

If a Sister shall fix her eyes on one of the

other sex, or if she shall utter an improper word.

If any Sister shall take without permission what is assigned to the use of another Sister, though with no intention of keeping it, or shall absent herself without leave, and without any cause whatever, from Chapter, sermon or from the common Dormitory at night, or if she shall go out of the Convent without leave.

For these and such like faults, there shall be imposed in penance, fasts, disciplines, psalms and venias, as shall seem just, according to the number and degree of the faults.

If a Sister accuse herself of a grievous fault, she should be treated with more indulgence, than if she had been proclaimed by another.

The habitual commission of any light or middle fault must be considered as amounting to a grievous fault.

313. The Sisters are not obliged to accuse themselves of such grievous faults as are from their own nature secret.

SECTION IV.

314. OF MORE GRIEVOUS FAULTS.

315. It is a more grievous fault if any one should be disobedient to her Superiors by contumacy or manifest rebellion, or shall presume insultingly to contend with them.

If any one shall openly rise up against her Prioress, or Superiors, by caballing, conspiracy, or malicious agreement. If, however, any one not maliciously, but in truth, shall see anything in the conduct of the Prioress, which it is not right or fitting to tolerate, let her make it known with prudence and charity to Superiors in higher authority.

It is also a more grievous fault if any Sister shall assert that the Prioress or Mother General are not lawfully such, and shall refuse them obedience, before Superiors shall have pronounced, in case of doubt.

If any Sister shall seriously trouble elections.

If any Professed Sister shall lay aside the religious habit without cause.

If any one shall procure for herself or another, by unlawful means, to be exempt from the authority of her Superior. Now a Sister would be guilty of this fault if she were to seek in any way, directly or indirectly, through the influence of any one not under the obedience of the Institute to obtain the revocation of any ordinance made concerning herself or another, or of any obedience enjoined on herself or on another, or to be placed in or removed from any Convent or Office; or if, for any cause whatsoever, she should appeal against any Superior or member of the Institute, to a tribunal foreign to the Institute, excepting only the Apostolic See, to which it is immediately subject, or should summon, or cause to be summoned, any Brother or Sister of the Institute before such tribunal. The same fault is incurred by any Superior or Sister who shall renounce any privilege granted to the Congregation.

It is also a more grievous fault if any Sister shall maliciously strike another.

If any one shall take, with the intention of concealing it, anything which has been given to the use of others, or which belongs to the common stock, or if she shall keep anything as her own.

If any one shall have given or received little presents or other things without leave, or shall conceal the things which she has received.

If any one shall clandestinely send or receive, or read, or cause to be read to her, or to any one else, letters, or anything in writing, without leave expressed or presumed.

If any one shall falsely accuse another Sister of any crime, for which she would have incurred the penalty of the more grievous fault.

If any one shall report evil of the House or the Sisters, or reveal any important secret to an extern, or if she shall commit any capital crime.

316. The penance due to the more grievous fault, is incurred by her who shall commit (which may God forbid) a breach of her vow of chastity, which sin ought to be punished more severely, and is to be abhorred above all. If, however, her fault be not publicly known, her conduct shall be examined in secret, and suitable penance shall be imposed, as the circumstances and the person shall require.

317. For such faults as these, she who has been found guilty shall ask pardon, lamenting the grievousness of her sin, and she shall be

penanced according to the judgment of her Superiors. If the fault be of such a kind as to require the full penalty, she shall be the last of all in the Community, so long as her penance shall continue. She shall not eat at the common table with the rest, but in the middle of the Refectory on the bare ground.

At the Canonical Hours, and at grace after dinner, she shall lie prostrate before the door of the Choir whilst the Sisters go in and out. No one, without permission, shall presume to hold communication with her. So long as she is in this penance, she shall not be received to the kiss of peace; she shall not be put down for any Office of the Choir, nor shall any obedience be given to her, nor shall she have any voice in the Chapter, except in self-accusation, until she shall have made full satisfaction.

The Prioress, however, lest she should fall into despair, shall send to one who is in this penance, Sisters who shall exhort her to repentance; encourage her to patience; comfort her by marks of compassion; animate he to expiate her fault, and help her by their intercession. The whole Community shall, likewise, intercede for her if she give token of true humility.

Nor shall the Superioress refuse to show her mercy as far as lies in her power.

318. It is to be observed that, though to be kept separate from the Community be part of the penance assigned to the more grievous fault, yet it may also be enjoined for lighter faults than these.

SECTION V.

319. OF THE MANNER OF PROCEEDING AGAINST THOSE GUILTY OF MORE GRIEVOUS FAULTS.

320. It must be borne in mind that no one can condemn a Sister to the penalties of the more grievous fault unless sentence has been formally passed against her. Should such a case ever arise, the Conventual Prioress must immediately refer it to the Mother General, who will judge, with the advice of her Council, whether the case is sufficiently grave to be formally brought before the Ordinary. In all cases of more grievous fault, judgment, is never passed without written proceedings, under authority of the Chief Superior. After sentence has been passed, the dispensation from depriving penalties (*i. e.*, loss of rank and

of the active and passive voice, and inability to certain offices), is reserved to the same authority; but the Local Prioress can show all charitable indulgence in. dispensing from the positive penalties (such as fasting, etc.), adjudged to these faults, and must not enforce them with too much rigor; and they may even be entirely dispensed by the Mother General, if she judge it expedient.

321. No Superioress can declare herself absolved from her office, whatever transgression she may have committed.

322. Sisters who are under the penalty of the more grievous fault must on no account be assigned to small Convents, but to large ones, where they can better devote themselves to regular observance. And the Prioress of the Convent to which such Sisters are sent, must receive full information concerning them.

323. If the penance be condoned, the Sister is held to have made full satisfaction, and is free from all penalties, both privative and positive, and restored to her former rank.

Nevertheless, those who have once been condemned to the penalty of the more grievous fault ought not, in prudence, to be raised to posts of superiority; unless, perhaps, after many years, it should be clearly evident that they have changed for the better.

324. Those who have conspired against authority, and who have grievously and openly given scandal, must hold the last place in the Congregation, during their whole life, even after they have accomplished their penance; and if they are restored to their rank of Profession by legitimate dispensation, they still remain incapable of the Office of Prioress, sub-Prioress, or Vicaress, and they cannot be admitted to any election, nor to treat of the affairs to be submitted to the General Chapter, without special permission of the Competent Authority.

SECTION VI.

325. OF THE MOST GRIEVOUS FAULT.

326. The most grievous fault is when a Sister is incorrigible, that is, when she is not afraid to commit faults, and refuses to bear the penalty for them. If so extreme a case should ever arise, recourse must be had to the Sacred Congregation of the Propaganda, by means of the

Ordinary, for the purpose of obtaining from the Holy See the expulsion of the offender.

But Superiors are seriously admonished and entreated, to be mindful of the maternal charity and meekness which they profess, and to leave nothing untried whereby they may gain the souls of such of their subjects as seem almost to have fallen into the depth of evils, before they have recourse to the terrible and extreme remedy of expulsion; remembering that, should any soul perish through the misgovernment of negligent or indiscreet Superiors, Our Lord Jesus Christ will not fail, in the day of judgment, to require the blood of such souls at their hands.

SECTION VII.

327. OF APOSTATES.

328. If any one, having been guilty of apostasy, shall return of her own accord, asking for mercy, she shall on no account be received to remain permanently without the permission of the Mother General.

If she be received, she will be subject to the penalty of the more grievous fault, in proportion to her past offense, and present signs of repentance.

329. By appstasy is understood a rash departure from religion, with the intention of not returning. But, if any one goes away and returns immediately to the Institute, she does not incur the penalties imposed by the Constitutions for this fault.

330. Apostates, when received back, everywhere take the last place; and if their rank in the Congregation be restored to them by lawful dispensation, the years they spent in apostasy, and the years they spent in penance, must not be reckoned; so that they must rank, from the day of their restoration, below all those who have attained a greater age in the Congregation than they had when they left it. And even if they should be restored to all the privileges of the Order, they can never be raised to any post of Superiority.

Chapter XVIII.

SECTION I.

332. OF THE OBLIGATION OF HOLDING CHAPTER, AND ITS IMPORTANCE FOR REGULAR DISCIPLINE.

333. If the Chapter of Faults cannot be held every day on account of the occupations of the Sisters, it ought to be held at least once a week, or once a fortnight at farthest; at which Chapter, Superiors are obliged, not only to recommend the benefactors to the prayers of the Community, but also to hear the faults of their subjects, at least of one side of the Choir, if the Community is large, under pain of deposition from office. This obligation, therefore, is not fulfilled, as was declared at the Chapter of Rome, A. D. 1650, by correcting

the faults of the Religious in a passing way, as it were; but the Community must be assembled, at the sound of a bell, in a place set apart for the purpose, where the prayers to be said at Chapter may be conveniently recited, the faults of each Sister heard, and salutary penances imposed.

It rests, therefore, on the conscience of the Mother General, in the day of Jesus Christ, that she should labor with all zeal and diligence for the execution of this most salutary ordinance, on which depend the extirpation of bad habits and the correction of the Sisters.

334. No Sisters, of whatever quality or condition they may be, ought to absent themselves from the Chapter of Faults, except those who are seriously ill or indispensably occupied. And these latter ought either to ask leave before the Chapter to stay away, or at least, after the Chapter, within the space of one day, to declare the cause of their absence.

335. Those Sisters (Conventual Prioresses excepted) who are staying for more than a week in a Convent of the Congregation to which they are not assigned, ought to assist at the Chapter of Faults, and there accuse them-

selves, unless the Superioress shall otherwise appoint.

336. In this Chapter the Sisters should accuse themselves of their exterior faults committed against the Rule and Constitutions. If they do not accuse themselves of such faults, or if they omit to perform the penance imposed upon them, they dispose themselves to sin, and even fall into it.

337. It must be observed, that many of the faults enumerated in the sections preceding, such as using insulting language, telling a willful lie, breaking the fasts of the Church without cause and without permission, and the like, are faults not only because they are forbidden by the Constitutions, but also because they are evil in their own nature, or contrary to the law of God, or of the Church.   Hence, whoever transgresses such precepts, incurs a double penalty, both against the Law of God, and against the Constitutions.

338. Superiors must take the greatest care not to correct their subjects with passion, but to show all mildness and religious kindness toward them.

339. The proclamations which are com-

monly made in Chapter are of light matters
and are rather intended to remind the Sisters
of the faults which they have forgotten, than
as accusations or denunciations; and therefore
they may be made without any previous
admonition in private. But when the fault is
of such a nature as to injure the character, if
any one were to publish such a fault of
another Religious, without having first given
her private Sisterly correction, she would offend against the precept of our Lord, "*If thy
brother shall offend against thee, go and rebuke
him between him and thee alone,*" as St. Thomas
teaches. These proclamations, therefore, made
without preceding admonition, ought to regard
such things only as are contained in the sections
on light and middle faults, and should not be
made of the more serious faults contained in
the section of the grievous fault. But there are
two cases, when, as St. Thomas teaches, the
Sisters are not bound to observe the precept of
secret admonition even for grave faults; first
when the sin is public, and secondly, when,
though secret, it tends to the corporal or spiritual injury of others; for in these cases, whoever thus sins, sins not only against herself, but

against her neighbor, and therefore omitting private correction, they should at once proceed to denunciation, that such injury be prevented; unless, perhaps, they are firmly persuaded that such evils can . be immediately hindered by secret admonition. But, if the sin is public, a remedy must be applied, not only that the person who has sinned may become better, but also for the sake of others to whose knowledge her sin has come, that they may not be scandalized. And therefore such sins are to be publicly corrected

340. It follows clearly from what has been said, that a Sister is still less bound to accuse herself publicly of faults which affect the character, unless they were publicly committed.

341. The Sub-Prioress, generally speaking, is not to be proclaimed in Chapter.

342. The Sisters ought not to accuse themselves in Chapter of interior faults, nor of the interior motives of their exterior faults.

343. The Chapter of the Novices is held in the same manner as that of the professed Religious. The simple Novices accuse themselves in presence of the professed Novices, as they are seldom sufficiently numerous for it to be

expedient for them to have a separate Chapter. They go out before the professed Novices accuse themselves.

344. In order that the Sisters may assist at the Chapter of Faults with greater readiness and fervor, the Sovereign Pontiff Paul V., granted an indulgence of three years, and as many quarantines, to all those who, with a contrite heart, shall accuse themselves in Chapter, making at the same time a Spiritual Communion, and practising some act of virtue.

SECTION II.

345. OF THE MANNER OF HOLDING THE CHAPTER OF FAULTS.

346. When the Sisters have entered the Chapter Room, the Superioress who is holding the Chapter, says *Benedicite;* and at the answer, *Dominus*, all incline. Then after the benefactions that have been received, have been recited, and the intentions that are to be prayed for have been recommended to the prayers of all, the Prioress shall say: *Retribuere*, etc. Then the Psalms, *Ad te levavi* and *De Profundis*, shall be said by the Community, with *Kyrie*

eleison, Pater noster, etc.; the Hebdomadaria shall say the three Versicles : *Oremus pro Domino Papa,* etc.: *Salvos fac servos tuos et ancillas tuas,* etc.; *Requiescant in pace;* with these three Collects : *Omnipotens sempiterne Deus, qui facis mirabilia,* etc.; *Prætende,* etc.; and *Fidelium,* etc.; after which the Sisters shall sit down. Then the Superioress shall say, with brevity, whatever may seem to her necessary for the maintenance of good discipline and for the correction of the Sisters ; after which she shall say, " Let those who are guilty of any faults make the *Venia,*" and immediately those who are conscious of having committed faults shall ask pardon by prostrating upon the ground. If the Novices are to be heard in Chapter, their faults shall be first heard, and when they have gone out, the other Sisters, rising, shall humbly confess their faults.

347. The Sisters must never speak in Chapter, but for one of the following reasons : either to tell their own faults, to proclaim those of others, or simply to answer the questions of their Superiors. Whilst one Sister is standing and speaking, no other Sister shall speak.

348. No one must proclaim another merely

on conjecture, nor from hearsay, unless she mentions the person from whom she heard it, and that person be present in the house.

349. When the faults have been heard, the Prioress says, *Adjutorium nostrum*, etc.; and so the Chapter ends.

END OF PART FIRST.

PART SECOND.

OF THE GOVERNMENT OF THE CONGREGATION.

CHAPTER I.

350. OF THE AMERICAN CONGREGATION OF THE MOST HOLY ROSARY.

351. The American Congregation of the Most Holy Rosary of the Third Order of St. Dominic, comprises all the Convents of women hitherto founded, or hereafter to be founded, in these United States, in dependence on the Mother House of St. Clara's, Sinsinawa Mound, Wisconsin.

352. We are, moreover, united under the care and jurisdiction of one General Superioress, bearing the title of Mother General,

whose power and rights are defined and limited.

353. Each branch House is governed by a Local Superioress.

354. The Mother General shall reside at the central House. In her absence, the Vicaress General shall supply her place.

355. The Congregation has one common Novitiate, and a common administration of funds.

356. The expenses incurred for the common good of the Congregation must be defrayed by all the Houses.

357. Each House of the Congregation shall contribute according to its means, to the support of the Novitiate which is at the Mother House.

CHAPTER II.

358. OF THE MOTHER GENERAL.

SECTION I.

359. OF THE OFFICE AND AUTHORITY OF THE MOTHER GENERAL.

360. The Mother General is canonically elected by all the Vocals of the General Chapter She must have completed ten years from her religious Profession, and must be at least thirty-five years of age. Her term of office shall last six years, after which she cannot be confirmed unless she obtain two thirds of the votes, and the confirmation of the Ordinary, who, as Delegate Apostolic, ought to preside over the Chapter. She cannot be re-elected for a third term without an interval of six years, unless by dispensation.

361. The Mother General everywhere holds the first place in the Congregation; and in whatever Convent of the Congregation she

may be, she says the *Fidelium*, *Adjutorium*, etc., and rings the little bell in the Refectory.

362. The Mother General has the power of proposing to her Council the names of those whom she considers most suitable for the office of Conventual Prioress; and then the election is made by secret suffrage.

363. The Mother General has power, after consulting her Council, to appoint Vicaresses for those houses which are not yet erected into Priories.

364. She has also power, with the consent of six Mothers of Council to absolve a Conventual Prioress from her charge before the expiration of her term of office, in order to appoint her to the government of another Convent.

365. She can, with the advice of her Council, nominate to every other office in the Congregation, excepting those reserved to the Diffinitory of the General Chapter.

366. She can depose, change or transfer the Sisters, Sub-Prioresses and other officials. But for the deposition of a Conventual Prioress before the expiration of her term of office, the consent of the Council is required.

367. She must convoke the General and Intermediate Chapters at their appointed times. The General Chapter elective shall be celebrated every six years; and the Intermediate, which is called the Assembly, in the third intermediate year.

368. At the expiration of her term of office, the Mother General governs the Congregation as Vicaress General, until the confirmation of the new Mother General.

369. In case of the death or removal from office of the Mother General, the Conventual Prioress of the Mother House of St. Clara's, Sinsinawa Mound, shall act as Vicaress General.

SECTION II.

370. OF THE ELECTION OF THE MOTHER GENERAL.

371. It belongs to the Vicaress General, when there is no Mother General, to assemble the Electresses for the election of the new Mother General.

372. Those who have a right to vote in the election of the Mother General are the following:

1. The Vicaress General.
2. Ex-Mothers General.

3. The Conventual Prioresses of the Congregation.

4. The Associates of the Conventual Prioress, canonically elected by the Conventual Chapters of their respective Communities.

5. The Mothers of Council of the Congregation.

373. If any of the Electresses are absent when the election is at hand, they must be summoned. But if they cannot come, the others may canonically proceed to the election in their absence.

It is prohibited for absent Electresses in any election to vote by letter or by proxy; but they must be personally present in the place of election, unless they be sick in the same Convent, and then the Scrutineers must go to them to receive their votes.

374. Twenty-four hours before the election, the Electresses must be called to the place of election by the sound of a bell, and a public *Tractatus* must be held, in which the list of eligibles shall be read, the necessary qualifications for a Mother General shall be pointed out, the hour fixed for the election on the following day, and leave given to the Electresses,

but to no others, to communicate with each other for mutual information on the subject of the election. Those who have no right of voting must not presume to mix themselves up with the election, in word or writing, either by themselves or by others.

375. The President of the General Chapter shall be the Ordinary of the place, or his Sub-Delegate, where the said Chapter is held: he shall preside over it as Delegate of the Holy See, and shall give the absolution of faults to all the Vocals, if possible, the day before the Election. On the day of Election, the Vocals shall receive Holy Communion.*

376. The Mass of the Holy Ghost ought to be said or sung in the Convent where the election is to take place.

377. The Electresses being all gathered together at the sound of a bell, at the hour and in the place appointed, the President of the Chapter must make a protestation that he has no intention of admitting any one who ought not to be admitted, or of excluding any one who ought not to be excluded. The grace of

* The Electresses, on the day of Election, must receive Holy Communion, under pain of being deprived of the active voice. By the active voice is meant the right of electing.

the Holy Ghost must be invoked by the hymn *Veni Creator*, with its versicle and prayer, as prescribed in the Processional.

Then the three Scrutineers must go to the table. The Scrutineers for this Election are the three Conventual Prioresses who have longest worn the habit of the Order. The Vicaress General, even though she should happen to preside at the Election, must not sit on the bench, nor act as Scrutineer, unless she be one of the three above-named Prioresses.

378. With regard to the Scrutineers, to make the matter quite clear, the cases must be determined, in which one of the Scrutineers by right would have to be replaced by another; and the rules to be observed, for each of these cases, must be explained. The cases are five in number:

1. When the Electresses wish to add a fourth Scrutineer.

2. When one or more of the Scrutineers renounce their office of Scrutineer, but not their vote.

3. When the Scrutineers renounce both their office and their vote in the Election.

4. When one of the Scrutineers by right is absent.

5. When one of the Scrutineers is, in the judgment of the majority, incapable of exercising the office of Scrutineer, on account of some defect of sight, or of hearing, or some difficulty in writing.

In the first and second cases, a Scrutineer must be elected by the plurality of open and public schedules, even though the number of votes be below the half; and if the number of votes be equal, the eldest shall be Scrutineer. In the third and fourth cases, the eldest Prioress, after the one who is absent, or who has renounced her vote, shall be Scrutineer without any election. Finally, in the fifth case, a Scrutineer must be elected by secret votes; and it requires the majority above the half, for a Sister to be elected. The Scrutineer in every canonical election, must always, under pain of nullity, be taken from the body of electors.

379. In obedience to the decree of the Council of Trent, every Electress must write, or cause to be written, on her schedule, the name of the person she elects; but the name of the Electress must never be written, nor

must it be revealed to the Scrutineers, or to the Confirmer.

· 380. When the three Scrutineers, have sat down at the table in presence of all, they shall first place their own votes, and then receive those of the others, written on folded schedules, in a vase or urn, being attentive to no other thing than that one schedule only be brought by each Sister and deposited by her in the urn. And that this may be done rightly and without fraud, no Electress shall put her hand into the urn along with the schedule, but she shall drop in one schedule only from above, so that the Scrutineers may see it as it falls. The Scrutineers must then go to receive the votes of the sick, if there be any.

The Scrutineers having received the votes of all, must empty out the folded schedules on the table in the presence of all, and count them and see if their number is equal to the number of the Electresses; and if their number is not found to correspond with the number of the Electresses, the schedules shall be immediately burnt, without being unfolded or read.

But if the number shall be found to be correct, they shall unfold them, read them, and write them down in secret, after having rendered them visible one by one to the President of the chapter only. They must then burn the schedules, in presence of the Electresses, before the publication of the scrutiny.

381. When a Sister is not of the number of the Electresses, it suffices for her election that the number of votes she obtains should exceed the half; thus, supposing the Electresses to be five, three votes would suffice for her. But if she belongs to the number of the Electresses, the case is different; for, as it is not lawful to vote for one's self, it is necessary that the elect in this case should have such a number of votes as would still be a majority, subtracting her own vote, if, perchance, she had voted for herself.

382. If any blank schedules be found in the scrutiny, or any which are conditional or uncertain, or which name a person who is obviously and indispensably deprived of the passive voice, no such schedules are to be counted, when the Electresses are numbered to determine how many votes are required for a true election.

383. After all the votes have been taken down in writing, the Scrutineers, coming into

the midst of the Chapter Room, shall publish the names of those who have had votes, and express the number of votes which each one has had; which must be done even if no one has been elected by the majority above the half, that the Electresses may be guided in a second scrutiny.

384. If it should happen that even in the third scrutiny, the Election is not successful, there shall be a fourth, between the two who have received the greater number of votes in the third scrutiny; and if there is still an equality of votes, the President shall choose one of them, whom he shall cause to be proclaimed Superior-General; afterward giving notice of it to the Sacred Congregation of the Propaganda.

385. If there is an election, after having first published the scrutiny, the first Scrutineer, holding in her hands the Book of the Constitutions, must, in the place of all the Electresses, form the decree of election, saying: " I, Sister N., in my own name, and in that of all the Electresses present, elect Sister N. as Mother General of the Congregation of the Most Holy Rosary, of the Third Order of St. Dominic." And this she must say, even though she have not herself

voted for her. If the first Scrutineer has been elected, the second Scrutineer must take her place in publishing the scrutiny and forming the decree. The process of election must then be written down in full, stating the number of Electresses, the number of votes obtained, as well by the elect as by others, and that nothing was omitted of those things required for a canonical election. This document must be subscribed with the name of the Scrutineers, closed, sealed in presence of all before they depart from the place of election, and shall be confirmed by the President, and the Election shall be made known to the Sacred Congregation of the Propaganda.

386. The Sister who is canonically elected cannot at once renounce her right, but is bound to wait until the Confirmer has canonically pronounced on the subject. And if he should refuse to confirm the election, she cannot appeal, because such election confers no right.

387. The whole Community are then called to the Chapter, and the name of the elect having been published, the Chantress begins the Psalm *Laudate Dominum omnes gentes*, and the Community continues the Psalm with the

Gloria Patri, the right choir singing the first verse, which is ended without *Pater Noster.*

· 388. The election of the Mother General cannot take place until the previous Mother-General is altogether removed from office.

389. If the Mother General shall die before the first Sunday in June, even if it be in the first year of her Office, the Vicaress General is bound to convoke the Chapter for the time of the vacancy, near the Feast of St. Dominic, unless her Council decide not to urge it

SECTION III.

390. OF THOSE WHO ARE ELIGIBLE TO THE OFFICE OF MOTHER GENERAL.

391. For a Sister to be capable of being elected to the office of Mother General, the following conditions are required:

1. She must have completed ten years from her Profession.

2. She must be at least thirty-five years of age.

3. She must not have been sentenced to the loss of the passive voice, on account of any fault.

4. She must not be sister to the Mother-

General immediately preceding; and if such a one should be elected, the election would be null and void.

5. She must be able to join the Community in the Choir, the Refectory, the Dormitory, and all the other acts of regular life, in a becoming manner. It was ordained by Pope Clement VIII. of happy memory : " Let those chiefly be elected to offices, dignities and posts of Superiority, who are able and wont to observe the Rules and Constitutions of the Order, especially in all that relates to the service of the Choir, and to the common food and clothing."

SECTION IV.

392. OF THE DURATION AND CESSATION OF THE OFFICE OF MOTHER-GENERAL.

393. The Mother General elect, as soon as she has received her confirmation, is bound to accept or refuse the office within the space of three hours after she receives the notification of her election; and she must with her own hand write the day and hour of her acceptance on the letters-patent of confirmation, in presence

of two witnesses; and the accepted letters must be read before the whole Community of the Convent in which the elect is present, and must be subscribed by the person who reads them publicly, noting down the day and hour. The confirmation is given by the President of the Chapter, as Apostolic Delegate, with the obligation of sending the act of election·and confirmation to the Sacred Congregation of the Propaganda.

394. The authority of the Mother General begins upon the day on which she accepts the confirmation of her office; nevertheless, in order that the General Chapters may always be celebrated at their appointed time (unless in case of death or removal from office), her term of office begins with the Chapter of Election, and lasts six years.

395. This period of six years is to be understood as meaning from one General Chapter to the next, without regard to a few days or even months, which sometimes, according to different circumstances, may be either wanting to, or in excess of, the exact period of six years.

The office of the Mother General and her authority always terminate with the day imme-

diately preceding that on which the Diffinitresses of the General Chapter are elected, and
on which the consultatory deliberation is held
respecting the new Mother General to be elected
on the day immediately following.

396. If a Conventual Prioress should be
elected Mother General, as soon as she has
received and accepted the confirmation of the
election, she shall be held to be absolved from
the office of Prioress, even if such absolution
be not expressed in the letters of confirmation.

397. The newly-elected Mother General is
earnestly exhorted in the Lord to make a spiritual Retreat before entering upon her charge.

398. The Mother General on going out of
office, must deliver to her successor a full
account of the state of the Congregation. She
must also see that the letters and the Acts of
the Sacred Congregation of the Propaganda,
and all other important papers, are carefully laid
up in the Archives of the Congregation.

399. At the General Chapter, her term of
office having already expired, she must render
an account to the Diffinitresses of receipts and
expenditures, both as regards her person and
her office.

400. After the expiration of her term of office, she remains of right a Mother of Council of the Congregation, and has a voice in the General Chapter. She cannot choose her own place of residence, but remains in all respects subject to her successors in the government of the Congregation, and to the Conventual Prioress of the Convent to which she is assigned.

SECTION V.

401. OF THE DUTIES OF THE MOTHER GENERAL.

402. The Mother General, as the true Mother and Superioress of the whole Congregation, should watch with maternal vigilance over the spiritual and temporal needs of each and all of her children. She should encourage the Sisters to place a filial confidence in her, and to have recourse to her for comfort in all their troubles. She must take care that they have free access to her at all times, either in person or by letter

403. She must enter on her office in the fear of God, having recourse to Him by humble prayer. She must not be hasty to introduce novelties, and if she must make any changes,

she may not do it, until she shall have acquired by experience, full knowledge of the state of the Congregation, the Convents, and the Sisters. In governing the Congregation, she must take counsel with the more discreet, who fear God and are zealous for religion. She must avoid as far as possible all party spirit, and beware of being influenced by motives of personal affection or familiarity.   .

404. She must labor with all her strength to maintain perfect observance throughout the Congregation, as well with regard to the three essential vows of religion, as to the due supply of food and clothing of the Sisters, and the proper care of the sick ; lest for want of those things which necessity requires, any should be led to fall into the vice of appropriation. She must, moreover, be vigilant concerning the Office, that it be duly recited in the manner prescribed, both in and out of Choir, and that all be present at it who are able ; and she must provide the Convents, as far as possible, with competent Chantresses. She must see that all who are able, take their meals in the common Refectory, and not in rooms apart.

405. In all these things, mindful of the

manner of acting of the Sovereign Master who
first began to do and then to teach, she must,
with all diligence, promote exact observance,
not by word of mouth only, but yet more by
her own example. These injunctions receive
new force by the Apostolic authority of Pope
Clement VIII., whose words are as follows:
" We admonish all Superiors in the Lord that
they remember the account which they will
have to give, at the last day, of the flock
entrusted to them ; therefore with all zeal let
them be watchful that those things which have
been wisely and piously enjoined in the Rules
and Constitutions of their Order, concerning
mental prayer, silence, fasts, the Chapter of
Faults, and other spiritual exercises, be observed to the letter; and let them understand that on these, as on their foundations,
the edifices of all religious Orders are to be
built up." (25th July, A. D. 1599.)

406. The Mother General must not easily
absent herself from the Office, especially from
Compline, unless perhaps on account of bodily
weakness, or urgent business.

When she is in Choir, she holds the first
place on the right side.

She must take her meals in the Refectory or Infirmary. She must not allow any notable singularities to be provided for her at table.

407. The Mother General ought especially to have at heart the interests of the poorer and more distant Convents, and she must help them as far as she is able, both by assigning to them a competent number of Sisters, and in other ways. She must animate the other Communities to assist them, and must often comfort them by her letters and, when necessary, with visits also, and encourage them in all good.

408. Until the Congregation is divided into Provinces, the Mother General is bound by herself, or by deputy, to hold a Visitation in every Convent of the Congregation three times, or at least twice, during her term of office (or oftener, if necessary); she will inquire into the general state of the House, the observance of Rule, the administration of funds and temporalities, for which purpose, she will carefully examine the accounts and books of the House, the state of the Schools, and manner of teaching, etc. She will also have an interview with each of the Sisters, and endeavor, with prudence and charity, to remedy the grievances which

may exist, and to promote the general happiness and good. She may stay in each House, as long as she thinks necessary, to inaugurate and carry out any changes or ordinances, which she has made in her Visitation. It shall be the duty of the Mother General to transmit, at the end of every three years, to the Sacred Congregation of the Propaganda, the personal, economic and disciplinary state, both of the Novitiate and of the Institute.

The manner of opening, proceeding with, and closing the Visitation, will be determined by usage.

409. The Mother General has power to nominate the Mistress of Novices, to admit Novices to Profession or reject them, to accept foundations, to authorize or prohibit expenses, for building or the like, but in all these she cannot act without the vote of her Council (excepting always the power of the Sacred Congregation of the Propaganda, where it may be necessary), whose decision she is bound to execute, so that any of the above-mentioned acts performed by her without their vote or contrary to their decision, would be null and and void.

410. The Mother General must keep a Book

called a Register, in which she must note down all her principal acts.

SECTION VI.

411. OF THE VICARESS OF THE MOTHER GENERAL.

412. The Mother General, with the advice of her Council, may appoint a Vicaress, if she shall judge it expedient, to assist her in the government of the whole or part of the Congregation, whose authority expires at the death or removal from office of the Mother General.

413. If, for any urgent cause, the Mother General should have to take a journey beyond the limits of her jurisdiction, she is bound to leave a Vicaress, with full authority to act in her stead; which authority, however, expires as soon as the Mother General returns, unless the latter should otherwise- ordain. But if, before her departure, she appoints no Vicaress, the Prioress of the Mother-House of St. Clara, Sinsinawa Mound, shall act as Vicaress.

414. When the Mother General is within the confines of her jurisdiction, she ought not to confide the office of Vicaress, either over the whole or a part of the Congregation, to one

who is actually holding the office of Conventual Prioress, unless perhaps for a time, and from some urgent cause.

415. A Vicaress thus appointed has the full power of the Mother General in the houses which are made subject to her jurisdiction; but she cannot appoint or deprive the Conventual Prioresses. Within the jurisdiction assigned to her, she says the *Fidelium*, and holds the first place on the left Choir. But the Vicaress General of the Congregation, when there is no Mother General, has the full authority of a Mother General, and everywhere holds the first place on the right Choir.

SECTION VII.

416. OF THE APPOINTMENT OF THE SISTERS.

417. No one can be received into the Congregation on condition of being assigned exclusively to any one Convent, and never being moved to any other; but all the Sisters can be moved from one Convent of the Congregation to another at the will of their Superior General until there are Provinces.

418. These appointments must be made by

the Mother General; but it is the duty of the Superioress of the Convent which a Sister is leaving, to provide her with sufficient money for the expenses of the journey, and with her full allowance of clothing.

419. In making these changes, the Mother General should always consult with the Superioresses of the Convents from which the Sister is to be removed, and to which she is to be sent, and must show all such consideration for their wishes and convenience, as is compatible with the general good.

No subordinate Superioresses must presume to delay or resist any appointment that may have been made by the Mother General.

420. The letters of appointment shall be addressed to the Superioress of the Convent to which a Sister is to be assigned, and read publicly to the Community of that Convent. This publication efficaciously transfers the appointment of the Sister from her former Convent to the second, with the rights of election and of suffrage that follow from it.

421. The Mother General must not be too easy in sending Sisters by way of deputation (that is, on a visit) to Convents to which they

are not assigned; and, if sometimes this has to be done, the deputation must be restricted to a short time, unless when a Sister is sent to another Convent on account of sickness.

If a Sister is thus deputed to a Convent, she must exercise the office of Hebdomadaria in her turn, follow the Choir, attend the Chapter of Faults, if her stay be prolonged beyond a week (unless she be a Conventual Prioress), and discharge all other duties, as though she were assigned there.

422. Sisters who are deputed, even beyond a day's journey, must be summoned to the elections of the Convent to which they are regularly assigned.

423. The Mother General alone can give permission for any Sister to go from one Convent to another, unless in case of some urgent necessity, and then she must be informed as soon as possible. But this rule does not apply to those Convents which are so near each other that the Sisters can easily go and return on the same day.

SECTION VIII.

425. Besides such· visits as the Mother General makes to the Convents from time to time, she shall make a regular Visitation of each Convent, as prescribed by the Constitutions, in person, every two, or, at least, every three years.

426. The ceremonies to be observed at a Visitation are as follows: At an appointed time, the Sisters shall be called to Chapter, and there the Mother General shall succinctly declare the points on which she wishes to hear the Sisters, namely :

1. The manner of performing the Office and other spiritual duties, including the Chapter of Faults.

2. The observance of silence and other points of regular discipline.

3. All that regards poverty, common life, and the administration of the Convent revenues.

4. The care of the sick.

5. The administration of all the offices of the Convent.

6. The state of the material buildings.

7. The Schools and other charitable works of the Community..

8. The provision of food and clothing.

9. The relations of the Community with externs.

10. The Inventories and other important books.

In all these inquiries, it must be the object of the Mother General to maintain throughout the Congregation that uniformity of observance in which the beauty of religious life consists; so that the outward uniformity which is thus preserved in our customs may both represent and maintain that inward union of hearts which ought to exist among us.

427. Superiors and Visitors should be very cautious not to reveal the names of those from whom they have heard the faults of others.

428. The Visitation must not be unnecessarily prolonged. No exact time can be assigned for hearing the Sisters; it suffices that they be heard with diligence and solicitude, so that time be not needlessly wasted. When the Mother

General has heard all the Sisters, beginning with the youngest, she must correct whatever she finds amiss, either privately, or in Chapter ; but this correction of faults, after all have been heard, cannot be prolonged beyond three days, which days should be continuous.

429. The Mother General may make ordinances at her Visitation, which should be left in writing, and which remain in force till the next Visitation.

430. If the Mother General be unable to make the Visitation in person, she may appoint a Deputy, whose powers shall be expressed in her letters, which she shall read in Chapter before opening the Visitation. A Visitor so appointed keeps the rank of her Profession, except whilst holding the Chapter of Visitation.

431. When the Mother General has herself made a Visitation of any Convent, she should not send a Deputy the same year, except in case of great necessity.

432. Those who are appointed as Visitors should be grave and mature in character.

CHAPTER III.

434. The Members of the Council of the Mother General (or Council of the Congregation) are :

1. The General Bursar of the Congregation.

2. Four Mothers elected by the General Chapter.

Those Mothers elected by the General Chapter must be thirty-five years of age, and must have accomplished ten years from their Religious Profession, They may be chosen from the entire Congregation. It is desirable that six of the Mothers of Council should, if possible, be resident at the Mother-House of St. Clara's, Sinsinawa Mound.

435. In the event of the death of a Mother of Council elected by the Chapter, or her appointment to a Priory, or of her becoming in any way incapacitated from fulfilling her office, the Mother General, with her Council,

may, if necessary, provide another till the next Chapter.

436. It must be borne in mind that, whenever there is question of instituting a Conventual Prioress, at least four Mothers of Council must be present, under pain of nullity. And should it not be possible to assemble that number in the Mother-House, other Sisters duly qualified must be chosen to fill the place for that occasion only.

437. At every meeting of the Council, there must be at least five present, including the Mother General, or whoever presides in her place.

Nevertheless, if the subject under discussion relates to the Novices, the Mistress of Novices must always be admitted, besides the Councillors.

438. The Council can deliberate only when it is convoked by the Mother General or her Vicaress; and that, in her presence, or in the presence of a Sister who holds her place with her consent. Nor can the Council deliberate òn any matters except those which have been proposed for deliberation by her who lawfully presides over it.

439. In affairs of less importance, it is often advisable for the Mother General to ask the advice of her Council ; but she is not always obliged to follow it. In certain important affairs, however, to be hereafter specified, she cannot act except with the consent of her Council, given under pain of nullity, by secret suffrage, with black and white beans, or something of the kind. When, therefore, any of these serious matters have to be discussed, the Mother General is bound to give notice beforehand to the Mothers of Council, that their decision may be the more mature.

440. Before the Council, the *Anthem* "Come, O Holy Spirit," etc., shall be said, with its *V. R.* and Prayer ; and after the Council the Prayer, " Prevent, we beseech Thee," etc. At the Meeting of the Council, the Mother General shall lay the question before the Mothers, after which each one may modestly give her opinion. In holding Council, after stating the case, and giving the requisite explanations, the Superioress must give her Councillors opportunity of speaking with perfect freedom, and do her best to secure the sincere expression of their respective opinions on the

question on hand.   But the matter can be decided only by secret suffrage, as has been said.

When the votes have been taken, they must be publicly poured out before all, so that each of the · Mothers can easily see and count them.

In all affairs thus decided by the Council, a simple majority of votes suffices.

No one can vote by proxy ; but, if a Mother of Council be sick, it is allowable to go to receive her vote.

A Secretary shall be present, elected by Mothers of Council, by secret suffrage.   If she is not of the number of the Mothers of Council, her vote is not decisive, but consultative only.   She is, however, bound to secrecy, like all the Mothers of Council.   She shall enter all the subjects of deliberation with their decision in a register.   The entry shall be signed by the Mother General and by the Secretary.

441. The important affairs, for which the Mother General necessarily requires the deliberation and consent of her Council, are chiefly the following :

1. The appointment or removal from office of the Mistress of Novices.

2. The appointment or removal of the General Bursar of the Congregation.

3. The appointment or removal from office of Mothers of Council.

4. The appointment or removal from office of the Secretary of the Council.

5. The nomination of two Examiners, who are to examine those who are to be received to Clothing and Profession. (These two Examiners must be chosen from among the Mothers of Council of the Congregation, or at least from among the Mothers of the Conventual Council of the Novitiate House.)

It is to be observed that, in all these and similar nominations, the Mother General proposes a name; and after discussion, the Mothers of Council give their votes by secret suffrages.

442. The following is a list of yet more important affairs :

1. The appointment or removal from office of a Conventual Prioress.

2. The undertaking of a new foundation.

3. The undertaking of any new institution involving grave responsibilities.

4. The undertaking any new building or considerable additions or repairs.

5. All borrowing, mortgages, or alienation of immovable property.

6. Purchases and other important investments of capital.

7. The dismissal of a Novice before Profession.

8. The Reception of Sisters to Profession. The permission of the Bishop of the diocese is also required, both for receiving Novices to the Habit and to Profession.

443. If any one of the Mothers of Council shall in any way reveal the secrets of the Council to the prejudice of justice, or of correction, or of any person whatsoever, she shall be deprived of her office of Mother of Council, nor can she ever again be a member of the Council, except by dispensation of the Mother General with her Council.

444. In all cases the Mothers of Council should avoid speaking of what has taken place at the deliberation of the Council; and even when the matter decided on becomes public, they must not refer to what passed in Council on the subject.

445. The Mothers of Council of the Congregation are entirely subject to the local Super-

iors ; and are in no way exempt, in virtue of
their office, from any Community exercise, or
from the Chapter of Faults.

446. In Convents which, under some liter-
ary or religious title, have been incorporated
by a law of the State, the Sisters who shall
form the Board of Trustees shall exercise all
the powers granted to them by the State Char-
ter; but to avoid an unnecessary number of
officers, five Sisters who are elected Members
of the Council shall be appointed Trustees of
the Corporation ; and those who shall for any
cause, cease to be Members of the Council, shall
resign the office of Trustee. The Members of
this Board of Trustees shall be chosen by the
Mother General, with the consent of her Council.

Chapter IV.

SECTION I.

447. OF THOSE WHO HAVE A VOICE IN THE GENERAL CHAPTER, AND OF THE TIME OF ITS CELEBRATION.

448. The General Chapter shall be held every six years. The time assigned for the General Chapter is the Saturday preceding a Sunday occurring between the fourth day of August, Feast of our Holy Father, St. Dominic, and the fifteenth day of August, Feast of the Assumption.

449. Those who have a right to sit in the General Chapter are the Conventual Prioresses with their Associates, canonically elected by the Vocals of their respective Convents; the Mothers of Council of the Congregation, and Ex-Mothers General.

450. The General Chapter is presided over

by the Mother or Vicaress General, unless the Ordinary of the place presides, as happens for election.

451. Four Diffinitresses shall be elected, who shall treat of all the affairs of the Chapter, and decide upon them, with the Mother General.

452. The election of the Mother General belongs regularly to the General Chapter; but, if it should happen from any cause that no election is to take place, the celebration of the Chapter is nevertheless not to be omitted.

SECTION II.

453. OF THE ASSOCIATE OF THE CONVENTUAL PRIORESS.

454. The Associate of the Conventual Prioress at the General Chapter, has a vote in the election of the Mother General, if made in that Chapter.

455. Each house has a voice in the General Chapter; and if there be five Sisters who have a right to vote, the Prioress not included, the Convent may send an Associate of the Prioress to the General Chapter. No Convent can

elect an Associate unless there be five Vocals, not including the Prioress.

456. By Vocals are meant those who have the active voice; that is, the right of voting in this election. For a Sister to possess the active voice in this election, the following conditions are required:

1. She must have completed six years from her Profession.

2. She must not have been deprived of her voice for any fault. No one can be excluded from an election under pretext of any fault, unless she have been deprived of her voice by sentence of lawful authority, and that at least a month before the time of election.

3. She must have been assigned to the Convent where the election takes place at least two months before the day of election.

4. She must not, in consequence of a new appointment, have voted for an Associate of a Prioress the same year in another Convent, unless she be appointed Sub-Prioress of the Convent to which she is newly assigned.

: 457. No appointment and changes of the Vocal Sisters can be made within two months of this election, unless for some grave cause;

and, if any such should take place, they shall have no effect, either as to loss of voice in the Convent from which a Sister is removed, or gain of voice in the Convent to which she is assigned. If the Mother General shall be found to have failed in this point, she shall be judged by the General Chapter.

458. Although the number of Vocals ought not to be increased within two months of the time of an election, yet this is not to be understood as excluding any one who, within those two months, completes six years of Profession.

459. For a Sister to be eligible to the office of Associate, the following conditions are required :

1. That she have fulfilled seven years from her Profession.

2. That she have not been deprived of the passive voice for any fault.

3. That she be assigned to the Convent in which she is elected, though she may happen to be absent at the time of the election.

4. That she be not the Sub-Prioress, in order that the Convent may not be deprived of the presence of both Prioress and Sub-Prioress at once ; but the Sub-Prioress may be elected if

the General Chapter is to be celebrated in her own Convent, or if her term of office will expire before the Chapter, and another Sub-Prioress can be appointed and be present in the house before the Prioress leaves for the General Chapter.

460. It belongs to the Sub-Prioress to appoint the day for treating of all that relates to the election of the Associate of the Prioress, and of the business to be sent to the General Chapter, and to preside at both. The Prioress must take no part in the election of her Associate.

461. The form of election is the following :

1. There is no Votive Mass of the Holy Ghost.

2. The Vocals are not obliged to receive Holy Communion on the morning of the day of election.

3. The Scrutineers are the Sub-Prioress and the two eldest Sisters among the Electresses. If the Electresses wish to choose a fourth Scrutineer, or if one or more of those who are Scrutineers by right, renounce their office, but not their vote, another must be elected by open schedules ; and she who has the

largest number of votes is chosen. If the votes are equal, the elder in the Order shall be Scruti-neer. If the Scrutineers renounce their office and their vote in the election, or if one of those who are Scrutineers by right be absent, the eldest in the Order after the one who has re-signed, or who is absent, shall be Scrutineer, without any election. If a Scrutineer have a difficulty in seeing, hearing or writing, which, in the opinion of the majority, hinders her from exercising the office of Scrutineer, another Scrutineer must be chosen in her place, by secret suffrage, the majority of votes above the half being required for her election. The Scru-tineers must always be chosen from among the body of the Electresses.

4. If, after the first three scrutinies no one is elected, whoever, at the fourth scrutiny, has a majority, though not above the half, shall be held to be truly elected; and if in this last scrutiny two Sisters shall have equal votes, the elder in Religion shall be considered as lawfully elected.

5. The process of election has not to be re-corded at length, since the office of Associate needs no confirmation.

6. The Community is not called together to receive the announcement of the election.

7. After the publication of the election to the Vocals, testimonial letters shall be written, signed by the Scrutineers, closed and sealed in presence of all, before they depart from the place of election ; and these letters shall be delivered to the Sister elected, who must take them with her to the Chapter; and without them she cannot be admitted to a voice in the Chapter, unless her right can be fully ascertained in some other way.

462. If, after her election, the Associate should happen to be prevented from going to the Chapter, the Convent may elect another in her place.

463. The Associate has a vote only in the General Chapter of the year for which she was elected. If, from any cause or hindrance, the General Chapter should be omitted that year, she cannot be admitted in virtue of such an election to the General Chapter of the following year. In like manner, if the election of the Mother General should have to be made more than once, an Associate must be elected anew by the Convent for each election, unless the

news of the annulling of the election should arrive before the dissolution of the Chapter.

SECTION III.

464. OF WHAT IS TO BE DONE THROUGHOUT THE CONGREGATION AT THE APPROACH OF THE GENERAL CHAPTER.

465. The Mother or Vicaress General must be careful to convoke the Vocals of the Chapter in due time. When the General Chapter is held in the interval between the Feast of St. Dominic and Feast of the Assumption, as usual, the Convocation should be made on the first Sunday in June.

She must also enjoin such prayers as she shall think fit throughout the whole Congregation, for the happy election of the future Mother General and the blessing of God upon the Chapter.

466. When the General Chapter is at hand, the election of the Associate of the Conventual Prioress must take place in all the Convents of the Congregation. There shall be also a deliberation in each Convent concerning those matters which are to be referred to the General

Chapter. From this deliberation the Conventual Prioress is altogether excluded. This deliberation must not be prolonged beyond one day. But the election of the Associate of the Prioress may be held on another day, if it shall please the Vocals.

467. The Mother or Vicaress General must require of the Conventual Prioresses a complete statement of the condition of their Convents as to observance, health, charitable works, temporal means, etc., which returns must be sent in at least a month before the Chapter, that the Mother General may be enabled to draw up a complete report of the state of the Congregation to lay before the Diffinitresses of the Chapter.

468. When the time for the Chapter is at hand, the Prioresses must not omit to go to it; and the Mother General, with the Diffinitresses of the Chapter, shall compel to be present those Prioresses who absent themselves from the General Chapter on slight cause. Those Sisters who are not Vocals shall not come to the Convent where the Chapter is being held, unless with special leave from the Mother General.

469. No petition can be presented to the

General Chapter from a Community, unless it has been approved by the Chapter of that Convent. This is to be understood of petitions made in the name of the Convent, not of individual petitions.

SECTION IV.

470. OF WHAT IS TO BE DONE IN THE CONVENT WHERE THE CHAPTER IS HELD, IMMEDIATELY BEFORE ITS CELEBRATION.

471. Before the Vocals proceed to the election of the Diffinitresses and the celebration of the Chapter, the Mother or Vicaress General, with the advice of the Mothers of Council of the Congregation, shall appoint Examiners, to whom it belongs to inspect and approve the testimonial letters of the Vocals. These Examiners shall refer all grave doubts to the Mother General and her Council, who shall determine the validity of the votes by secret suffrage, and not otherwise.

472. The Vocals being approved, they shall proceed to the election of the four Diffinitresses, on the day immediately preceding that assigned for the Chapter. Their authority and

privilege of place date from the time of their
election. If there is to be an election of a
a Mother General, there may be, on this same
day, if it is thought good, a consultatory deliberation respecting her election, which can take
place only one day before the election.

SECTION V.

473. OF THE ELECTION OF THE DIFFINITRESSES.

474. By Diffinitresses of the General Chapter are understood four Sisters, who are canonically elected by all the Vocals of the General
Chapter, and to whom it belongs to deliberate
and decide on all the business of the Chapter
(a few matters alone excepted), in concert with
the Mother General.

475. For a Sister to be eligible as Diffinitress in the General Chapter,the following conditions are required : -

1. She must have completed seven years
from her Profession.

2. She must not have forfeited her passive
voice by any fault.

3. She must not be the Mother General

whose term of office expired immediately before the Chapter.

476. Sisters who have no voice in the General Chapter may be elected as Diffinitresses, provided they are present in the house where the Chapter is held. In this case, however, they have no voice in the election of the Mother General, and are not to be admitted to that election; but they must be admitted to all the acts of the Chapter.

477. The Mother or Vicaress General presides at the election of the Diffinitresses; and the same form is to be observed as in the election of the Associate of the Conventual Prioress, with the following exceptions:

1. No consultatory deliberation is held.

2. The three Scrutineers by right are the Mother General or Vicaress General, the Prioress of the Convent where the election is held, and the Sub-Prioress of the same Convent (if she be one of the Vocals of the Chapter; for in every canonical election, the Scrutineers, under pain of nullity, must be taken from the body of the Electresses).

If one of these should be unable to act as Scrutineer, the remaining two will suffice. But if two of them should be disqualified, then their places must be supplied by the two eldest Vocals of the Chapter. If it shall please the Electresses, a supernumerary Scrutineer may be elected by open schedules.

3. The four Diffinitresses are not to be elected one after the other, but altogether, by schedules on which are inscribed, for the first scrutiny four names, and for the other scrutinies, if they are required, as many names as there still remain Diffinitresses to be elected. But if, in the first or subsequent scrutinies, more than four have an equal number of votes above the number required for an election, then those who are eldest in the Order shall be held to be lawfully elected. This election, like that of the Associate of the Conventual Prioress, necessarily terminates at the fourth scrutiny: so that she, or they who have most votes in the fourth scrutiny, even if the number be less than the half, shall be held to be Diffinitresses. It is not necessary that the process of election be written out, as the election of the Diffinitresses requires no confirmation, and takes effect immediately. The Com-

munity is then called to the Chapter and the names of the Sisters elected, published. ·

478. At the General Chapter during the term of their authority, the Diffinitresses take precedence of all the Sisters, even Prioresses, not only in the Chapter, but also in the Choir, in the Refectory, and everywhere; ranking among themselves, if they are Prioresses, according to the age of their Convents. They say the *Fidelium*, even in the presence of the Conventual Prioress. If there should be any-thing gravely reprehensible in the conduct or government of the Mother General, the duty of representing it to higher authority belongs to the Diffinitresses. The Diffinitresses are bound even after the dissolution of the Chapter, to keep the secret of the Diffinitory; and if any Sister should afterward be discontented with what has been there determined, the Diffinitresses must not excuse themselves (even in case one of them should not have consented to the act in question) by throwing the respon-sibility on the others, nor must they in any way reveal the persons whose votes or influence have decided the affairs which are made sub-jects of complaint.

SECTION VI.

479. OF THE MANNER OF CELEBRATING THE GENERAL CHAPTER.

480. When the General Chapter is held at the usual time, that is, on a Sunday between St. Dominic's Day and the Feast of the Assumption, the Diffinitresses must be elected the previous Friday; and if there is to be an election of a new Mother General, that election must take place on the Saturday, in the manner before explained. On the Sunday or Monday, the solemn celebration of the Chapter begins.

481. On that day, in the presence of the Mother General, of the four Diffinitresses, the Vocals of the Chapter, and the whole Community, the Holy Ghost must be invoked by the chanting of the *Veni Creator*, with the customary versicle and prayer. Then follows an instruction from the Superior presiding, which being ended, as the needy are to be helped as soon as possible, the names of the Sisters who have died since the last Chapter are to be first recited, and the appointed

prayers for the departed said. Should the
General or his Vicar have died since the last
Chapter, their names should be recited, as
well as those of any deceased Fathers or
Brothers of the American Province.

Then follows the recommendation of the
living.

After this, all who are not Vocals must with-
draw. Then a Chapter of Faults is held,
presided over by the Mother General. The
Diffinitresses shall accuse themselves in the
first place, and then the Vocals, beginning
with the highest in rank. All the penances
are given by the Mother General. Lastly, she
shall accuse herself, and receive a penance
from the first Diffinitress.

482. With regard to the various proceedings
in Chapter, there are some in which all the
Vocals of the Chapter take part, and some
which belong solely to the Mother General and
the four Diffinitresses.

483. It belongs to all the Vocals of the
General Chapter to elect canonically four
Mothers of Council of the Congregation and
the Bursar General in the same manner as the
Diffinitresses, the four names being written on

one schedule, and so put into the urn. The
Mothers thus elected must not be less than
thirty-five years of age, and ten years professed.

484. With this exception, it belongs to the
Diffinitresses, together with the Mother General, to deliberate and decide upon all the other
business of the Chapter. If in their decisions
they should divide equally, their opinion shall
prevail with whom the Mother General shall
agree; otherwise the majority shall prevail.
But if, from the addition or absence of the
Mother General, or from any other cause, the
sides shall be equal, they shall elect one of the
Chapter, and whichever side she shall take, her
opinion shall prevail.

485. Whatever is thus done by the Mother
General and the Diffinitresses, is to be under-
stood as having been done by the General
Chapter.

486. The Diffinitory shall elect the Mistress
of Novices.

Thirty years of age, and seven years of Profession, are necessary qualifications for the office
of Bursar General and of Mistress of Novices.

487. The Mother General whose term of
office has just expired, must render an account

to the Diffinitory, both of her official and personal expenditure.

488. The names of the Sisters deceased since
the last Chapter, with a brief notice of each
are to be inserted in the Acts of the Chapter.

489. The place and time must be appointed
both for the Intermediate Chapter, and for the
General Chapter next following.

490. The Diffinitresses are not to be hindered in their decisions. No Sister, of whatever rank or condition, shall make any exceptions, refusals, or protests against all, or any
of the Diffinitresses, to prevent them from proceeding with their decisions; and if any one
shall presume to act in contradiction to this ordinance, she shall incur the penalty of the more
grievous fault, and shall be excluded from the
Chapter, that the dissension may be expelled
with its author.

491. No one who is not a member of our
Congregation shall be admitted to the secrets
or deliberations of the Chapter.

492. During the Chapter, regular life must
be exactly observed, and all superfluities in
food must be avoided.

493. No one shall go out of the Convent

without necessity, and the consent of the Diffinitory ; and those who are obliged to go out shall return as soon as possible.

· 494. All the Vocals of the Chapter should be within call. A Sister shall be appointed to attend upon the Diffinitory, to summon any Sisters whose presence may be required. The room used by the Diffinitory must be kept locked in their absence.

495. The General Chapter should not be prolonged beyond eight, or at most ten days, which are computed from the day of the election of the Diffinitresses inclusively.

496. At the end of the Chapter, absolution of faults shall be given if possible.

SECTION VII.

497. OF THE ACTS OF THE GENERAL CHAPTER.

498. The Acts of the Chapter must be sent to the Sacred Congregation of the Propaganda as soon as possible to be revised, corrected and confirmed. They must not be promulgated to the Convents of the Congregation until they have received this confirmation ; and the Acts

·shall be promulgated according to such annotations and corrections as the Sacred Congregation of the Propaganda shall have made. After the Acts of the Chapter have been confirmed, it is the duty of the Mother General to promulgate them without delay.

Let all the Sisters accept with unanimity and devotion whatever has been regulated by the Chapter. Let there be no murmurs, protestations or contradictions.

499. The Ordinances of General Chapters begin from the time of their promulgation, and last, not only until the next Intermediate Chapter, but until the promulgation of the Acts of the next General Chapter is made in each Convent.

500. The Mother General cannot change or rescind the Acts of the General Chapter; and it is altogether forbidden for the Diffinitresses of the Chapter to grant her authority to do so. If a Mother General shall presume to change, diminish, increase, or in any way dispose, regarding said Acts, without just and needful cause, her whole proceeding shall be null and void.

501. The Acts of the Chapter shall not be

shown to those who are not of our Congregation, without reasonable cause and without leave of Superiors.

SECTION VIII.

502. OF THE INTERMEDIATE ASSEMBLY.

503. Three years after the General Chapter, an Intermediate Assembly shall be celebrated; in which, besides the Mother General, ex-Mothers General, Conventual Prioresses and Vicaresses only have a voice. In this Assembly, all things are treated of which relate to the common good of the Congregation. No Diffinitresses are chosen, nor has the Assembly power to draw up petitions in the name of the Congregation; but the Mother General must give an account of her receipts and expenditure, both personal and official. Any ordinances made by this Assembly expire with the promulgation of the Acts of the next General Chapter.

SECTION IX.

504. OF PRECEDENCE.

505. The following is the order of Precedence to be observed in our Congregation :

1. The Mother General or Vicaress General *in capite.*

2. The Vicaress appointed by the Mother General over the whole Congregation.

3. The Conventual Prioress in her own Convent.

4. Ex-Mothers General who rank among themselves according to the time of their Profession.

5. Conventual Prioresses out of their own Convents ; who, if there be more than one, rank among themselves according to the age of their Convents.

6. The Vicaress of a House not yet erected into a Priory, in her own House.

7. The Sub-Prioress in her own Convent. Nevertheless she retains her stall of Office in Choir, although ex-Mothers General and Conventual Prioresses be present.

8. The Mistress of Novices everywhere, if

she have actually under her charge six Novices. Nevertheless, for greater convenience, she keeps near the Novices in Choir, Refectory and Processions, but takes her place after the Sub-Prioress at Chapter and in the Council.

9. The Vicaress of a House out of her own House.

10. Sisters Professed, according to the time of their Profession.

11. Sisters not Professed, according to the time of their Clothing.

12. Postulants.

According to the order above set down, the Sisters will take their places in Choir, Refectory, Chapter and Processions, with the two ex ceptions above named.

506. When a Conventual Prioress holds the first place in a Convent where she has no juris-diction, as is noted above, she says the *Confiteor*, *Adjutorium*, *Requiescant* and *Fidelium*, and gives the blessing in Choir, but she does not give the signals for beginning the Office, etc. In the Refectory she has the place of the bell, but she neither rings the bell nor gives the signals, nor says the *Adjutorium*.

507. The Convents in our Congregation rank

thus: The Mother-House of St. Clara s, Sin-sinawa Mound, holds the first place; the others according to the date of their foundation.

508. When the General Chapter is held, the Diffinitresses, during the time their authority lasts, take precedence everywhere over the other Religious, as well Prioresses as other Sisters, the Mother General alone excepted.

Chapter V.

509. OF THE BURSAR-GENERAL.

510. The Bursar-General of the Congregation is elected by the Diffinitory of the General Chapter, and holds office for six years; but she may be proposed for re-election several times, if it seems expedient to the Mother General to propose her. She is by right a Mother of Council of the Congregation as long as she holds her office.

511. If the appointment of a Bursar-General should have to be made out of the General Chapter, the Mother General cannot appoint her of her own authority, as she cannot remove her of her own authority; but both these acts require the consent of the Council.

512. The office of the Bursar General is to administer the income of the Congregation under the direction of the Mother General. The income arises principally from the following sources:

1. Tuition fees of pupils in all Schools of our Congregation.

2. Interest on dowries of the Sisters, in whatever way invested.

3. Rents of houses or lands on which the capital of the Congregation has been spent.

4. Interest on legacies or property left to the Congregation.

5. Donations made to the Sisters.

6. Annuities, life interests, etc.

7. The surplus arising from the local revenues of the several Convents.

Out of this fund must be paid:

1. The usual expenses of the Congregation.

2. The annual interest on mortgages of Convent property and other loans, when the means of any Convent so burdened, are insufficient to pay them.

3. The monthly or quarterly allowance to assist those Convents of the Congregation, the local revenues of which are inadequate to their support, which allowance must be proportioned to the means of the Congregation and the necessities of those Convents.

513. Moreover, it is the office of the Bursar General to keep an exact account of the admin-

istration of the capital of the Congregation ; of
the investments of the dowries of the Sisters ;
of all expenses of purchases, buildings, etc.
But in questions relating to the administration
of capital, she cannot act on the authority of
the Mother General alone, but the consent of
the Council is also required, and in the cases
contemplated by the Canons, there must be
obtained the approbation of the Sacred Congregation of the Propaganda.

514. Every month the Bursar General shall
submit a statement of the receipts and expenditures to the Mother General in presence of two
auditors.　Every three months, she shall receive
from the Bursar of each Convent of the Congregation a statement of the receipts and expenditures of that Convent, drawn up under
certain principal heads ; and from these she
shall herself make out a general statement of
the receipts and expenditures of the whole
Congregation, to be submitted to the Council
of the Congregation at the end of the year.
And these yearly statements should be signed
by herself, by the Secretary of the Council, and
by the Mother General.

515. The account books in which these

statements are contained, as well as the daily account books of the Bursar General, should, when finished, he carefully preserved in the Archives of the Congregation.

516. It is also the duty of the Bursar-General to see that each Religious possessing property shall conform herself to the Rules of Poverty before established.

Chapter VI.

518. In the Mother-House of St. Clara's, Sinsinawa Mound, there should be a room set apart for the keeping of the Archives of the Congregation.

519. A Sister shall be appointed by the Mother General, and her Council to act as Archivist. Her office shall last for three years, after which she may be re-appointed.

520. The Archives shall be closed with two different keys, one of which shall be kept by the Mother General, and the other by the Archivist.

521. In the Archives shall be preserved the deeds and documents relating to the property of all the Convents of the Congregation, and all papers of importance, such as Papal Rescripts, and grants of Indulgence, etc., referring to the whole Congregation, the letters of the Ordinaries, the Patent or Diploma of aggrega-

tion to the Order of St. Dominic, the letters of institution of the Mother General, the Acts of the General and Intermediate Chapters, the Register of Acts of the Mother General, the Council-Book of the Congregation, the Book of Clothings and Professions, the finished Account Books of the Bursar General, Inventories of the more valuable property of every Convent, and the Annals of the Congregation.

522. An exact list shall be made of all the books, papers, and other documents contained in the Archives. This list shall be signed by the Mother General and given to the Archivist when she enters on her office; and the latter must keep it corrected and in good order, and give it up when she goes out of office.

523. No document must be given out from the Archives, except with the leave of the Mother General; and the Archivist must take a note, showing when and to whom such a document has been delivered.

524. Every year, in the month of January, the inventory of documents contained in the Archives must be verified and completed.

Chapter VII.

525. OF FOUNDATIONS.

SECTION I.

526. OF THE NECESSARY CONDITIONS FOR THE ERECTION OF A CONVENT.

527. No new foundations shall be undertaken without observing that which is expressed in the Bull, " Romanos Pontifices." The Mother General cannot petition for leave to make a new foundation, without the consent of her Council.

528. The Mother General with her Council, must carefully consider the number of subjects available for the new foundation and the resources at command, both for the first expenses of the undertaking, and for the future maintenance of the Convent ; and she must thoroughly satisfy herself that the new foundation, if carried out, will not weaken the existing Convents,

or be too great a drain on the resources of the Congregation.

529. After the site of a new foundation has been maturely considered, complete plans of the whole Convent, as ultimately contemplated, should be procured; and if practicable, a model of the entire house should also be made, so as to exhibit the whole interior arrangement. After this plan has been approved by the Mother General and her Council, it cannot be altered at the pleasure of any Superioress without grave reasons, and without reference to the same authorities.

530. Our Convents should be plain and simple, a point which should be the more carefully observed as being in accordance with the spirit of our Holy Father Saint Dominic; and no ornaments in the way of sculpture, pictures and the like, should be permitted, except such as contribute to devotion and edification.

531. In the houses which are already constructed, it shall not be lawful for the Prioress or Syndica to raise any notable building without the consent of the Council of the Convent and the permission of the Mother General and her Council. And any one who shall pre-

sume to do otherwise, shall be removed from her office; so that for the space of three years, she shall not be Prioress of that or any other Convent.

532. No foundation shall ever be accepted, to which are attached onerous conditions, or such as are inconsistent with the spirit of the Congregation or its Constitutions.

533. It is strictly forbidden both to the Mother General and her Council, to accept any house, until they know, by the testimony of capable Sisters sent to inquire into the matter, that the place is suited for the erection of a Convent.

534. No Convent shall be received which is not left to the free disposal of our Institute, conformably to our laws and constitutions; and if the contrary be done, the transaction shall be null and void.

535. No new foundations shall in future be made, without a fair prospect of at least partial support from local resources, either from endowment, or from some remunerative work, such as Boarding Schools, Day Schools, etc.

536. If among the Houses already accepted and inhabited by the Sisters, there should be

one, the position of which is found to be disadvantageous and likely to continue so, which cannot be easily maintained, and in which Religion cannot be well fostered, or the works of charity to which the Sisters are devoted, suitably carried on, the Mother General may, with the consent of her Council, give up and leave such House when this can be done advantageously.

537. When a new foundation is undertaken, the Sisters assigned to it should be exemplary, grave and mature, and should at once begin without fail to keep Choir, Refectory, and the other observances of Community life.

538. No House should be erected into a Priory until it has supported six Religious for a year, and unless it be fairly provided with such buildings as are necessary for religious observance.

Chapter VIII.

539. OF THE CONVENTUAL PRIORESS.

SECTION I.

540. OF THE INSTITUTION OF THE CONVENTUAL PRIORESS.

541. The Conventual Prioress is elected by the Mother General and her Council.

542. The Conventual Prioress must be at least thirty years of age, and seven years Professed. This office lasts three years, at the end of which term she may be re-elected once, but she cannot be elected for a third term without an interval of three years, unless by dispensation.

SECTION II.

543. OF THE AUTHORITY AND DUTIES OF THE CONVENTUAL PRIORESS.

544. The Mother General is bound to appoint a Conventual Prioress within six

months from the day when the office becomes vacant.

545. Those only shall be chosen to fill the office of Prioress who are prudent and discreet, who know how to make themselves all to all, so that their subjects may be led by their example to observe the Rule and Constitutions of the Institute, and to be lovers of holy poverty.

546. Two sisters should not succeed each other as Conventual Prioresses in the same Convent.

547. No one can be elected Prioress who is not able to follow Community life in the Choir, the Refectory, and other exercises, and to sleep in the common Dormitory; and if any Prioress should fall into so weak a state of health as to be almost continually prevented from following Community life, and attending in Choir, and there seem no hope of her recovering her health and strength within the space of six months, she is bound to resign, and if she should fail to do so, she ought to be absolved from her office by the Mother General.

548. The Prioress-elect, as soon as her election is announced, is bound to accept or refuse

it within three hours after receiving the notification; and she must sign the letters of appointment with her own hand, in presence of
two witnesses, stating the day and hour on
which she accepts.   On the arrival of the
Prioress at her own Convent, the accepted
letters shall be read before the whole Community in Chapter or Refectory, and shall be
signed by the person who thus publicly reads
them, adding the day and hour.   The three
years' term of office of the Prioress expires on
the recurrence of that day and hour on which
her letters of appointment were accepted before
two witnesses.

549. Those who are newly appointed to the
office of Prioress are earnestly exhorted to
make a spiritual Retreat before entering on
the duties of their office.

550. As the Prioress by her office is raised
above the other Sisters, so should she also
precede them in the practice of every kind
of virtue.   She should, above all, practise
humility, and that the more fervently as she is
higher in authority, according to the counsel
of the Wise Man: " The greater thou art,
the more humble thyself in all things, and

thou shalt find grace before God." She must be assiduous in prayer, punctual in Choir, and at all other Community exercises exact in all that belongs to the observance of the Rule and Constitutions; in a word, she must render herself fit to be in all things a guide and an example to her Community.

551. She should animate her Sisters with fervor and sweetness to the practice of virtue, and strive with all her power to maintain peace and fraternal charity in the House, yielding sometimes to the counsel and wishes of others. She ought not herself to personally discharge any of the offices, and she should neither trouble the officials in the exercise of their charge herself, nor allow others to disturb them. She must be patient toward all, and receive all who wish to speak to her with sweetness, at any time whatsoever, but, during the time of deep silence, they should not disturb her except in case of great necessity.

552. In the Refectory she must avoid all singularity, and content herself with what is served to the other Sisters. She must follow the same rules as the rest with regard to clothing, and must banish both from herself and

others every kind of singularity and super-
fluity which could injure the perfection of the
Community, except what is really required for
the sake of health.

553. In case of sickness the Prioress shall
be taken care of with the rest in the Infirmary,
and the Mother General may charge some of
the Sisters, especially the Sub-Prioress, to see
that she takes the necessary rest and recreation.

554. The Prioress has authority over all her
subjects in all things which are contained either
explicitly or implicitly in the Rule and Constitutions. She may, therefore, make Ordinances,
either by word of mouth or in writing, for the
good government of her Convent, which Ordinances may be either maintained or altered as
circumstances may require, by those who shall
succeed her in the charge.

555. The authority of the Conventual Prioress in all that regards dispensation has been
already explained in the Prologue. (No. 16-23,
Section III.)

556. It is the duty of the Conventual Prioress to provide the Community, as far as she
is able, with clothing, and with sufficient food

properly prepared, above all in fasting seasons, that the Sisters may be the better able to fast. She shall especially watch with maternal solicitude that the aged, the infirm, and the sick have all the indulgences which are necessary.

557. She must provide the Sisters of her Convent who may have to travel, with sufficient money for the expenses of the journey.

558. The Prioress must cause the Constitutions to be read in the Refectory on the days appointed.

559. She must be careful to have an inventory kept of the things belonging to every office in the Convent, and she is bound to see that each Sisters on entering into office, receives the inventory of the things belonging to her office, and that the Sisters every year submit to her a list of the things given to their personal use.

560. She must not herself administer the revenues of the Convent, or exercise the office of Syndica, and she must see that the laws of the Deposit are strictly observed.

561. The Conventual Prioress must show an example of obedience and be careful to introduce no changes in customs long established in

the Congregation, without previous reference to the Mother General. Let her aim in all things to preserve that outward uniformity of custom which ought to be observed in all our Convents, in order to promote interior union of heart throughout the Congregation. The mainten-ance of this union of hearts, the greatest bless-ing that God can bestow, chiefly depends upon the efforts of the Prioresses. Let every Con-ventual Prioress, therefore, consider it a sacred duty to maintain this union, by cherishing in her Community a filial reverence for the Mother General, a sisterly cordiality and confidence to-ward all other Convents of the Congregation, and such charitable disposition as shall render each one ready to make any personal sacrifice for the common good.

562. It is the duty of the Conventual Prior-ess to superintend carefully all the existing in-stitutions attached to the Convent, and to see that the rules approved for these institutions are strictly observed. She should hold frequent examinations of all the schools, either in person or by some competent deputy.

563. The Prioress must be careful to see that the religious habits of the Community are

always made of the approved form and quality of material, of which patterns must be kept in the Archives, agreeing with those preserved in the Archives of the Mother-House.

564. She must not undertake any new works without the advice of the Council, and the consent of the Mother General.

565. She cannot be absent from her Convent for twenty-four hours, and that on most urgent business of the Congregation, without the permission of the Mother General, if possible. And each case of absence and its cause is to be immediately notified to the Mother General.

566. The Prioress must take care to provide the sick with food and medicine, and everything of which they stand in need; she is also bound to hold the Chapter of Faults at least once a fortnight; if she be found negligent in either of these respects she would be liable to deposition from office.

The Prioress is forbidden under the same penalty to undertake any notable building, or any great expense, without leave of her Superiors.

567. If any furniture of the Convent becomes superfluous, the Prioress must not dispose of it

in any way, even to another Convent of our Congregation, without the permission of the Mother General.

568. If any Conventual Prioress shall be found to be grossly negligent in the duties of her office, she should be absolved from it by the Mother General; but this can be done only on the conditions above mentioned. (No. 362.) When the Mother General gives letters of absolution to a Prioress, she must name in them a day not far distant, after which she shall cease to be Prioress. A Prioress who has been thus absolved from her office cannot be re-appointed to the same charge that year.

569. In the following cases the term of office of the Conventual Prioress is prolonged:

1. If the three years come to a close after the first Sunday of June, the term of office is extended till the conclusion of the General Chapter or Intermediate Assembly, if either of these is to be celebrated that year at the usual season.

2. If the General Chapter or Intermediate Assembly chance to be celebrated out of the usual season, that is between the fourth and fifteenth of August, and the Prioress' term

of office come to a close within two months previous to its celebration, her authority is prolonged until after the Chapter.

3. If the Congregation chance to be without a Mother General when the three years come to an end, the Prioress' term of office shall be prolonged until the election of the new Mother General, and the conclusion of the General Chapter, if, as is usually the case, the Mother General is elected at the General Chapter.

570. When her term of government is drawing to a close, the Conventual Prioress is bound, within the last month, to render an exact account of her administration to the Council of that Convent and to the Mother General, giving at the same time a faithful statement of the whole condition of the Convent and of its institutions. This written statement, signed by the Prioress and by all her Council, must be delivered to the Sub-Prioress, and a copy of it must be sent to the Mother General, to be communicated by her to the Diffinitory of the next General Chapter.

571. At the day and hour when the term of office of the Prioress expires, the Sub-Prioress

takes her place with the full powers of a Prioress, unless the Mother General shall have appointed some one else to govern it as Vicaress *in capite.*

. 572. The Mother General can appoint a Vicaress *in capite* over a Convent in the absence or even in the presence of a Conventual Prioress, who shall have authority even over the Prioress herself. But this must not be done unless from a most urgent cause, with consent of the General Council.

SECTION III.

573. OF THE VICARESS OF A HOUSE NOT YET ERECTED INTO A PRIORY.

574. The Mother General with the advice of her Council must appoint a Vicaress over each of those Houses which have not yet been erected into Priories, where the Community is small, and the Convent not fairly provided with what is needful for observance.

575. The Vicaress so appointed has the same authority in her House as the Conventual Prioress in her Convent.

576. The Mother General may remove her

from office at any time, and her authority expires at the end of three years, reckoning from the day and hour when, being present in the House, she began her government. The Mother General can appoint her for a second term, if she pleases; but after the expiration of the second term, the same Sister cannot be re-appointed till after an interval of three years, except by dispensation.

577. The authority of the Vicaress of a House does not expire with that of the Mother General by whom she was appointed.

578. The Vicaress always holds the first place in her own House, unless the Mother General, an Ex-Mother General, or a Conventual Prioress be present. In other Convents she ranks after the Novice Mistress.

SECTION IV.

579. OF THE CONVENTUAL COUNCIL.

580. In every Convent of the Congregation, certain prudent Sisters shall be appointed by the Mother General with her Council, who shall assist the Conventual Prioress by their advice

in matters of importance. It shall not be in the power of the Prioress to appoint or deprive them at pleasure, but this shall belong to the Mother General.

581. The Mothers of Council by right of office are:

1. Ex-Mothers General, if any be assigned residents in the House.

2. The Sub-Prioress actually in office.

3. The Syndica.

4. The Mother General can institute two or three Mothers of Council.

582. These Mothers of Council by appointment continue in office, unless removed, until assigned to another Convent, when the appointment ceases.

583. With regard to the manner of holding the Council, the election of a Secretary, the obligation of secrecy, etc., the same must be observed as in the Council of the Congregation.

584. The affairs to be treated of in the Council are:

1. The appointment or removal from office of the Depositaries, the Sacristan and the Syndica.

2. The leave given to a Sister by the local

Superioress (in a case of urgent necessity which gives no time for reference to the Mother General) to be absent from the Convent for a night unless it be to go to one of our own Convents in the immediate neighborhood. Except in such case of urgent necessity, the Conventual Prioress has no power to grant leave to any Sister to be absent for a night from the Convent, either to visit her own family or a Convent of another Order, or even one of our own Congregation, if distant; the right of giving such permissions being reserved to the Mother General.

3. The monthly and quarterly statements of receipts and expenditures.

4. The statement of her administration made by the Prioress before the expiration of her term of office.

5. Any important business that may arise.

585. For the following affairs the Conventual Prioress requires not only the advice, but also the consent of her Council, given by secret votes:

1. The institution of the Sub-Prioress, when, with the leave of the Mother General, she is to be chosen from that Community.

2. The absolution from office of the Sub-Prioress so appointed.

3. The appointment or removal from office of the Secretary of the Council.

4. The receiving any one gratuitously into the charitable institutions attached to the Convent; and if this is to be permanent, it further requires the sanction of the Mother General.

5. Any extraordinary expenses exceeding $10.

6. All matters which have to be referred to the Conventual Chapter. Nothing that has been rejected by the Council can be proposed to the Chapter.

586. The Prioress, without the consent of her Council, may incur expenses to the amount of $10, and with the consent of her Council to the amount of $100. But for any extra expenses beyond the sum of $100, the consent of the Mother General is required. These limitations are not to be understood as referring to the customary domestic expenses.

SECTION. V.

587. OF THE CONVENTUAL CHAPTER.

588. The Conventual Chapter which must not be confounded with the Chapter of Faults, consists of all the Professed Sisters assigned to the Convent, assembled together under the presidency of the Prioress, (or in some cases of the Mother General) to treat of certain affairs, which must of necessity have been previously examined and voted for by secret suffrage in the Council.

589. In the Chapter, though each one may modestly give her opinion, yet the question must be decided by secret votes, under pain of nullity. The votes must be afterward openly poured out, and so exposed that all the Vocals may judge of their number and quality; and at least three or four of the elder Sisters of the Community are bound to draw near and assist at the counting of the votes.

590. The matters which must be treated of in the Conventual Chapter are the following:

1. The alienation of anything valuable belonging to any particular Convent.

2. Any very important affair regarding the whole Community.

591. A Sister may, for grave reasons, abstain from giving her vote, but no one may vote by proxy.

592. The deliberations of the Chapter ought to be written down immediately in a book to be kept by the Secretary of the Council.

SECTION VI.

593. OF THE SUB-PRIORESS.

594. The Mother General ought to appoint a Sub-Prioress within a month from the time when the office became vacant. The Sub-Prioress may be chosen from the whole Congregation, and it is not necessary that she should have completed six years from her Profession. But if the Mother General shall leave the choice of the Sub-Prioress to the Conventual Prioress and her Council, they must choose amongst those Sisters only who are assigned to that Convent.

595. The Sub-Prioress cannot be deprived of her office, except by the same authority which instituted her.

596. The duration of her office is two years after which, if it please her Superiors, she may be re-appointed without any interval. But if, within the two years, a new Conventual Prioress shall be appointed, the Sub-Prioress may be absolved from her office if it seem good to the Mother General. If the term of office of the Sub-Prioress expire within two months previous to the expiration of the Prioress' term of office, she shall remain Sub-Prioress until the new Prioress is present in the House, and during that interval, she ought not to be deprived of her office, unless for some grave cause.

597. The Sub-Prioress must not be removed from office when the General Chapter is at hand.

598. The Sub-Prioress holds the next place to the Prioress in her own Convent, unless there be an ex-Mother General or the Conventual Prioress of another Convent staying in the House. Out of her own Convent, however, she takes the rank of her Profession.

599. The Sub-Prioress cannot be proclaimed in the daily Chapter, unless for some grave fault it shall seem expedient to the Prioress.

She is of right a Mother of Council of the Convent; and in the absence of the Prioress, she rings the bell in the Refectory, says the *Fidelium*, etc., and does all the other things that are reserved to the Superioress.

600. It is the duty of her office to be diligent about the Community, to correct those that do amiss, and to act in other things according as the Prioress shall appoint or permit.

601. As soon as she is appointed, the Sub-Prioress should diligently inquire of the Prioress, and bear in mind, what power she wishes her to have, as well in her presence as in her absence, and she must not go beyond what shall have been prescribed for her. She must be mindful of the regulations of the Conventual Prioress and the Mother General, and must take care that they are exactly accomplished by the Sisters. She must faithfully assist the Prioress, and not lend a willing ear to those who murmur and trouble others. It must be her constant aim to maintain a good understanding between the Prioress and the Community. She must reserve all matters of greater moment to the Prioress, and fre-

quently refer to her as to what is to be done. If anything notable should happen during the absence of the Prioress, the Sub-Prioress must report it to her on her return, even though it may have been corrected. She must also. remind the Prioress of what she has to do, if she has forgotten or is otherwise occupied, and she must give a faithful report of the state of the House and of the Sisters to the Mother General at her visitation. The Sub-Prioress ought to be almost always with the Community. She must take care that the signals for the various Community exercises are punctually given, that the Community never be needlessly kept waiting anywhere, and that all things be done in a becoming and orderly manner. She should, under the direction of the Prioress, arrange what is to be read in the Refectory.

When the Prioress is present in the House, the Sub-Prioress has no power of dispensation.

602. On the death or removal from office of the Conventual Prioress, the Sub-Prioress left in government is called Sub-Prioress *in capite*, and then she has the full powers of a Prioress until the new Prioress is present in the Con-

vent, and she can appoint a Vicaress to assist
her if she pleases. Nevertheless she must not
make notable changes in the Convent, and she
is bound to render an exact account of her administration to the new Prioress in presence of
the Council. Whilst the office of Prioress is
vacant, the Sub-Prioress must not undertake
any important transactions with regard to the
temporalities of the Convent, but must reserve
all matters of moment to the new Prioress;
unless urgent necessity should, in the judgment
of the Council, require the contrary.

SECTION VII.

603. OF THE SYNDICA.

604. The Syndica must be chosen from
among the more prudent and discreet Sisters.
Her duty is in conformity with the directions
of the Prioress and Sub-Prioress, zealously and
faithfully to take care of the temporal goods
of the Convent. She cannot, without a general
or particular leave, give away money, clothes,
food or anything else.

605. The Syndica is bound perfectly to
observe the laws of the Deposit, as explained

in the next section. It is advisable that all the money which comes into the Convent or goes out from it, should pass through the hands of the Syndica, who shall account for it to the Prioress and the Depositaries.

The Syndica must keep a book in which she shall enter her receipts and expenditures, day by day. At the end of each month or quarter, she should draw up a statement of receipts and expenditures, under certain principal and determined heads, which should be laid before the Prioress and her Council.

She must, every three months, draw up a similar statement of receipts and expenditures, to be signed by the Prioress, Sub-Prioress and Syndica, and forwarded to the Bursar-General of the Congregation, preserving an authentic copy in the Convent, in a book appointed for the purpose.

She must keep the bills, receipts, and other papers belonging to her office, in good order, and see that they are carefully preserved as long as they may be useful or necessary. She must also be most careful not to leave the money given to her charge exposed in such a way as to be a temptation to dishonesty.

Those who are negligent in providing necessaries for the sick must be removed from the office of Syndica.

Before giving an order for any alterations or repairs to any workman, let the Syndica be careful to have a proper estimate of the amount, to be laid before the Council.

Before going out of office, the Syndica must render an exact account of her past administration to the Prioress and her Council, and produce a correct inventory.

606. As the office of Syndica includes both the providing for the temporal wants of the Community, and the keeping of regular accounts of money received and expended, it may not be always possible to find one person possessing the necessary qualifications for both these duties. In that case, the office may be divided, one Sister providing what is necessary for the Community, with the title of Cellarer, and another, who shall be called the Bursar, keeping the accounts. But, as a general rule, it is much to be desired that the whole charge should be undertaken by one person, assisted, if necessary, by competent aids.

607. When the office of Syndica becomes

vacant, the Prioress is bound within a month, to appoint a new Syndica with the advice of her Council. But if there should not be any one in her Community competent for that office, she must have recourse to the Mother General, who will herself appoint some one to this charge.

608. No Prioress or Superioress of a House must, under any circumstances, herself exercise the office of Syndica; and, unless in case of absolute necessity, it ought not to be given to the Sub-Prioress.

609. The office of the Syndica lasts two years; but she may be reappointed with the permission of the Mother General.

SECTION VIII.

610. OF THE DEPOSIT, THE DEPOSITARIES AND OTHER OFFICIALS OF THE CONVENT.

611. In every Convent there ought to be a secure place called the Common Deposit, the key of which must always be kept by the Prioress. In this place there should be a box closed with three locks, in which shall be put all money from whatever quarter it may come;

and there must be three different keys, one of which must be kept by the Prioress, and the other two by two discreet Sisters, Motherr of Council, who shall be called . the Depositaries; and the officials of the Convent cannot spend money, under any pretext, unless it has been first placed in the Common Deposit.

612. Every week, or at least every month, the Prioress and the two Depositaries shall meet at the Common Deposit; when the Syndica shall render to them an account of the receipts of the preceding week or month; and she shall bring all the money she has received, to be laid up in the box of the Deposit, whence it cannot be taken out, except in presence of the Prioress and the Depositaries; and the sum so taken out must be immediately entered in a book kept for that purpose. When money is sent to the bank or drawn thence by check, it must be accounted for to the Prioress and Depositaries in the same way as that which is laid up in the Deposit.

613. The Bursar or Syndics cannot spend any money until it has been first brought to the Deposit, and thence consigned to her by the Prioress and Depositaries, unless in case

of some urgent payment which cannot be delayed; when it shall be sufficient to obtain permission from the Prioress, and to account for it afterward to the Depositaries. The Cellarer and Sub-Cellarer may fill the office of Depositaries, but not the Syndica or Bursar.

614. Accounts should be carefully kept by the Syndica, showing every item of receipt and expenditure, and also how far the expenses of the Convent are met by the local revenues; whether the Convent has been assisted from the general funds of the Congregation; or whether, on the other hand it yields any surplus to be paid to the general fund.

All money placed in the Deposit, or taken out from thence, must be entered in the Book of the Deposit.

615. Mothers of Council, Conventual Prioresses, and the Mother General must be vigilant over the exact observance of the laws of the Deposit.

616. It is forbidden to the Depositaries, under pain of deprivation of office, to reveal to seculars the state of the temporal affairs of the Convent or of the Congregation.

617. Deposits from seculars, must not, if pos-

sible, be kept in our Convents; but the persons should be advised to place them in Bank. If, however, in an emergency, a Deposit must for a time be received, proof should be obtained and preserved, in the hand writing of the person, of the amount deposited, and receipt taken of the amount when repaid. Such deposits, if they consist of money, must be placed in the Common Deposit; it shall not be lawful for any Sister, even the Prioress, to receive a deposit from any one, except it be so placed; and any one acting to the contrary incurs the penalty of the more grievous fault.

618. School fees paid weekly, small payments for work, etc., should be accounted for by the Sisters in their respective offices, either weekly or monthly, as the Prioress may direct.

619. The pocket money of the children in our Boarding Schools may, with permission of the Prioress, be administered by the Mistress of the School, without being brought to the Deposit; but in this case a careful account of such moneys must be kept and submitted to the Prioress.

620. It is forbidden to lend money, except in case of some pressing emergency.

621. The Seal of the Convent must be kept in the Common Deposit.

622. The Depositaries shall be appointed by the Prioress, with the advice of her Council. Their office lasts two years, but they may be re-appointed, without interval, with permission of the Mother General. The Sacristan, Infirmarian and Librarian are appointed in the same manner, and hold their respective offices for the same period.

SECTION IX.

623. OF THE ARCHIVES AND INVENTORIES OF THE CONVENTS.

624. In every Convent there ought to be, in some safe place, a cupboard for the Archives, where shall be laid up all the privileges, contracts, and other documents belonging to the administration of that Convent; the letters of institution of the Prioress and the Sub-Prioress, the ordinances of Visitors, the Acts of the General Chapters, the Council Book, the Chapter Book, finished Account Books, and any other important papers, with a correct inventory of the same. A plan of the water-pipes, gas-

pipes, and drains should also be kept in the Archives on which all fresh alterations should at once be correctly marked.

625. Every Convent should have a book, called the Book of the Great Inventory, which shall be kept in the Common Deposit. In it there shall be entered:

1. A list of all the privileges or other documents relating to the foundation and state of the Convent.

2. A list of the documents relating to the revenues administered by that Convent.

In another part of the same book shall be copied the inventories of all the offices of the Convent, leaving a sufficient number of blank pages between each for additions.

626. A correct inventory of all things belonging to her office must be given to each official when she enters on her charge, which she must sign with her own hand.

627. The Great Inventory shall be kept by the Archivist, and she shall revise it every year in the month of January, making the necessary additions or corrections on the right hand page, which must be kept blank on purpose.

628. All officials of the Community must perfect their inventories when they go out of office, making the necessary additions, and marking on the right hand pages, left blank for the purpose, any changes that have been made, or else making out a new inventory if requisite; and these inventories must be revised and perfected every year in the month of December.

629. Copies of the inventories of the Sacristy, the Library, and the chief valuables of each Convent, should be sent to the Mother General and should be corrected each year.

SECTION X.

630. OF TRAVELING.

631. No Sister can take a journey without permission from the Mother General.

She must have a suitable companion assigned her by her Superior; and from this companion she must not separate. The elder in the Order shall have authority over her companions, especially in what regards the journey, unless the Prioress shall have ordained otherwise.

632. If, for any grave reason, Sisters have to

remain out of their Convent for more than three days, besides the written permission, they must have letters of obedience to present in case of need, in which must be expressed the cause of the permission, either in general or particular, and the name of the place to which they are sent.

633. The Prioress is bound to supply a Sister with sufficient money for her journey.

The Sister who is traveling must take a direct road, and accomplish her journey in the time appointed.

If she should have to stop on her journey in places where there is a Convent of our Congregation, she is bound to take her meals and to sleep there, and not in the houses of seculars.

SECTION XI.

634. OF SISTERS WHO ARE ON A VISIT TO CONVENTS WHERE THEY ARE NOT ASSIGNED, AND OF GUESTS.

635. The Sisters who are on a visit in any Convent of the Congregation, should be kindly and charitably treated.

If they remain more than six days in the Convent, they are subject to the law of the Common Deposit, unless they be Conventual Prioresses; nor can they spend any money without permission from the Superioress in whose Convent they are staying. In this respect they are in the same position as those who are assigned to that Convent.

The Sisters who are staying in a Convent of the Congregation, even for a short time, are bound to exercise the office of Hebdomadaria, to follow the Choir, and to discharge other Community duties, just as though they were assigned there. If they are Conventual Prioresses, however, they do not attend the Chapter of Faults.

They are subject to the Superioress of the Convent where they are staying, and cannot go out without her leave.

636. The Guest-apartments of every Convent must be so arranged that secular visitors may be suitably entertained, without in any way mixing with the Community.

SECTION XII.

637 OF THE ANNALS.

638. Every Conventual Prioress must cause to be drawn up exact but concise Annals of all the important events connected with her Convent; and she must take care that these Annals are continued every year.

In like manner, the Mother General shall take care that the Annals of the Congregation be kept complete ; and she shall appoint a competent Sister who shall discharge this duty with zeal and fidelity.

Laus Deo
Beatæ Mariæ Virgini
Reginæ Sacratissimi Rosarii
Beato Dominico Patri nostro
et omnibus Sanctis.
Amen.